Windleaf

Windleaf

JOSEPHA SHERMAN

WALKER AND COMPANY
NEW YORK

First published in the United States of America in 1993 by
Walker Publishing Company, Inc.

Published simultaneously in Canada by Thomas Allen & Son
Canada, Limited, Markham, Ontario

Library of Congress Cataloging in Publication Data:
Sherman, Josepha.
Windleaf / Josepha Sherman.
p. cm.
Summary: In 1510 eighteen-year old Thierry, orphaned Count of Foretterre, undertakes a series of difficult challenges in order to free the half-human, half-fairy girl he loves from the hold of her cold-hearted father, Lord of Faerie.
ISBN 0-8027-8259-0
[1. Middle Ages—Fiction. 2. Fairies—Fiction. 3. Orphans—Fiction.] I. Title. II. Title: Wind leaf.
PZ7.S54575Wi 1993
[Fic]—dc20 93-615
CIP
AC

Printed in the United States of America

2 4 6 8 10 9 7 5 3 1

Contents

ONE

Ill Met by Moonlight

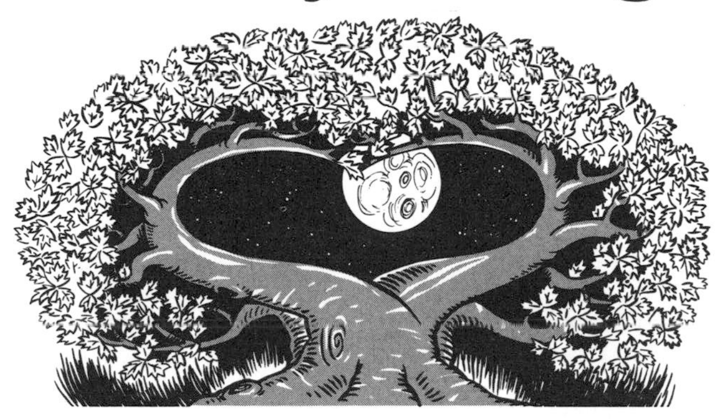

The forest was dense and old, its trees thick-trunked, its still, sweet-scented air rich with springtime and the hundred small chirping, whirring voices of the night. Clear, cold moonlight filtered down through the canopy of new leaves, liquid falls of silver through which Tiernathal moved with silent grace.

Tiernathal, Lord of Faerie—now reduced to merely lord of this small, sad band of exiles—was tall like all his race, lean almost to the point of gauntness, skin the clear white of someone who has never known sunlight. He was handsome in his own fierce, sharp-edged way, and old as mortals reckoned time, though his age was hinted at only in the weary, bitter green eyes. Long, silvery-fair hair swirled about his narrow face as Tiernathal stalked restlessly beneath this moon of mortal Earth.

Of all his people, he was the only one old enough or keen enough of memory to remember Faerie: that bright and wondrous land. There, the moon was pure, unstained, not like this shadowed imitation. There, no garish, poisonous sun spoiled the perfect sky that glowed with its own clear light. There, magic grew in every leaf and quivered in the very air—Tiernathal sighed softly, to him the list of wonders spelling simply *home*.

A home none of them might ever see again.

For one wild instant the sheer force of his despair broke free, savage enough to melt stone. But in the next moment it was gone, and the Faerie lord was falling back against a tree, gasping, eyes shut, cursing this mortal land, this *human* land, this land so weak in Power. . . .

How fair it had seemed once, so long ago, when he'd first found the Gate between the Realms, how deceptively fair when he and his people had wandered through, drawn by the novelty of mortal time. Of course this Realm had never been without its dangers. It had been impossible to ignore the twin perils of sunlight—which fatally burned pale Faerie skin—and worse, the monstrous substance known as "iron," that metal so alien to Faerie, so totally bound to Earth, that it destroyed magic and magic bearers at a touch. There had been the humans, too, the ugly, dirty, primitive creatures so quick to fear and hate. But they had been . . . manageable. Particularly after Tiernathal had taken a corner of the forest for his own, screening it with spells from sun and humankind, keeping it in safe, magical twilight, turning it to a place of quiet, shimmering beauty.

But I never thought to live in it forever!

Time had betrayed them. Unfamiliar with such a mortal thing, his folk had tarried here far, far too long, never realizing what was happening to them, never dreaming that, bit by tiny bit, the strength was slipping from them, sapped by this alien land. They had never been a fertile race, even in Faerie, and it was the marvel of them all that Tiernathal had sired not one but three children, three daughters. But those daughters were . . . lost to him. And not a child had been born to any of them since.

Worse, slowly, subtly, his people were losing magic, losing glory, losing the very essence of who and what they were. Soon they would be nothing more than memories to trouble human dreams. Tricked by that treacherous mortal Time, they had—even he, their liege lord—forgotten the way back to Faerie.

Tiernathal started fiercely forward once more, battling all

too familiar sorrow. But all at once he froze, alert in every sense, hearing the little night noises stop, feeling the still night air turn sharp with tension, recognizing:

"You," he said shortly.

"Indeed." The other voice was soft and deep, as though the earth itself had spoken, ever so slightly edged with warning, and leaves quivered as though in sympathy. "You wander far tonight, Faerie man."

"What I do or do not is hardly your concern."

As he spoke, Tiernathal scanned the forest with physical and psychic sight. But, as ever, even Faerie magic couldn't focus on the Other, on this mysterious entity that called itself only Forest Heart. Even Faerie sight couldn't catch more than the briefest, most tantalizing glimpses (hint of feather, glint of fang and fur) of this being that was the very life-force of the forest.

"But it *is* my concern," Forest Heart murmured, and the quiet leaves trembled again, without a breath of air to stir them. "This is my Realm in which you trespass, Faerie man."

Tiernathal bit back his anger. He knew only too well what elemental Power Forest Heart represented. His own Faerie magic was alien to this land, totally foreign in style and substance. But Forest Heart *was* the forest and its native, natural magic. As such, the being was far stronger than this Faerie foreigner, and they both knew it.

I will not fear you! Tiernathal thought, and hissed, "You are not my master, creature."

"You are not your own master," Forest Heart taunted. "Why do you stay here? Why?"

"Curse you, you know why!"

"Because you are lost, Faerie man, lost as any pathetic little human soul."

"No!"

A ripple of amusement stirred the leaves. "You hate to be compared to human folk, don't you?"

"They are inferior."

"Are they? You didn't always find them so. Not all of them. Not one in particular—"

Tiernathal tensed. "Stop it."

"Why? Have you forgotten her so soon? Have you denied her memory?"

"No, I—"

"Poor Faerie man. You've worked so hard to banish any soft emotions. You've even banished the ones most dear to you."

"I—Enough!"

"What's this? Afraid of truth? You, whose people never lie? Are you afraid of that one brief time of tenderness? Are you afraid to remember—"

"I am afraid of nothing!"

"Oh, but you are," Forest Heart taunted, but there was the faintest hint of something gentle behind the mockery, something sad. "Poor thing, poor thing, you've tried to banish love. Faerie man, Faerie fool, without love even Faerie magic has no strength."

"Has *this* no strength?" Tiernathal shouted. He hurled Power from him in a white-hot blast of fury.

But Forest Heart had already vanished in a quivering of leaves and an echo of laughter. Power shattered harmlessly against the ground and was gone.

Tiernathal hardly noticed. Aching with the memories the being had roused, he stood lost and alone and anguished in the moonlight.

TWO

A Day on the Farm

Thierry—Thierry Alain Gilbert, eighteen-year-old count of these lands of Foretterre in this year of our Lord 1510 and latest in a long line of counts—stood leaning lightly against the stone wall surrounding his family's rambling old mansion, breathing in the sweet spring air of this fine April day, looking out over his lands, hazel eyes warm with delight.

Spread out before him was a patchwork of neatly fenced fields rich brown from fresh plowing or already green with tender new growth. Beyond were the thatched roofs of Foretterre-the-Village, the newly whitewashed houses and small stone chapel surrounded by a riot of early flowers. Even the usually barren hill towering up to his left, beyond the estate's outer wall, had turned a pale apple green with new grass, and the three graceful birches on its crown were topped with delicate leaves. And beyond *that*, the vast, ancient forest was a tapestry in a hundred shades of green.

"Beautiful," Thierry murmured.

The count himself looked anything but noble just now, brown hair tied out of the way with a leather thong, and tall, lanky body clad in plain leather tunic and leggings like any common farmer. Hardly surprising: He'd spent the morning so far with farmers, the smell of freshly turned earth rich in his nostrils. The folk of Foretterre were free men, not serfs, though they did pay him rent in service and vegetables. They enthusiastically discussed the ongoing sowing of seed, the milking of cows, and the shearing of the communal flock of sheep with their noble landlord, smiling with him over the first of the new lambs and calves and agreeing that the estate's new bull, Goliath, for all his sour temper, seemed to be siring fine offspring.

Thierry glanced at that restlessly stirring mountain of animal. Goliath, densely muscled, large and dark as something out of a legend, was being moved from old pasture to new, towering over the men at his side. The Count moved uneasily forward to ask Hugo, his cattleherd, "You're sure you can transfer him safely?"

"Oh, easily, my lord. Once he smells the new pasturage—and his pretty ladies—why, he'll move smooth as cream."

Thierry nodded dubiously.

"A dark-souled creature, that," murmured a voice, and the count turned to see old Simon, his gardener, tall and thin as a pole topped by a wild thatch of gray hair, standing in the manor wall's doorway. Simon, Thierry often suspected, had a touch of what the peasants called feyness, and more than a passing acquaintance with the Old Gods. Eh, well, so did a good many of the Foretterre folk, despite all the efforts of Father Denis, the pragmatic village priest. When one's life revolved about the earth, Thierry thought wryly, one didn't worry too much about Heaven.

But Simon was blatantly eager to discuss his territory. If the man did, indeed, have any magic, it was with the manor garden, and his enthusiasm was contagious. Before he knew it, Thierry found himself on his knees beside the gardener, sun turning his hair to the exact color of the newly turned earth, amiably arguing with Simon over whether or not the lush new spring growth edging the manor's wall really was bean plants escaped from the garden.

A shout and an angry roar made them both look up with a start.

Goliath. The bull was most definitely not happy about

being moved, even with that bovine harem awaiting him. *Dark-souled, indeed,* Thierry thought. As the count watched, the creature tossed his head with a second roar, sending the men trying to hold him flying as though they were weightless. Goliath hesitated for a moment, as though stunned to suddenly find himself free, and pawed the ground uncertainly.

Now, if they only move gently, they can have him again before he makes up his mind. . . .

But one man's lunge was too quick for the bull's fragile temper. The animal charged, head down, horns glinting like curved blades. The servant yelped, throwing himself over a fence to safety just in time, the tip of one horn slicing through his leather jacket as though through gauze. Frustrated, the bull pawed the ground again, then thundered forward in a new direction.

"Lisette!" Simon gasped.

His tiny granddaughter, plump and happily dirty faced, had eluded her mother and wandered down from the manor through the open doorway. Too young to realize her danger, she stopped at the sound of her name, turning toward her grandfather with a toothless grin, heedless of Goliath.

"Oh, God, Lisette!"

That was the child's mother, Marie, rushing frantically forward out of the manor. But she was too far away, and everyone else seemed too stunned to move, so Thierry lunged into the charging bull's path, snatching blindly for Lisette.

Dear God, don't let me miss. . . .

His arms closed around the toddler. Her startled wail turned to frightened screams as Thierry tossed her brusquely out of the way. Willing hands caught her as the count's momentum sent him hurtling to the ground right in front of Goliath. Thierry twisted frantically even as he fell, desperate to scramble out from under those plunging horns. The bull's breath scorched him, hot as fire, the maddened eyes blazed into his own, he was never going to make it—

But then Goliath was brought up short as men caught him by the ropes dangling from nose ring and halter, too many men even for his strength. Gasping, Thierry staggered to his feet in time to give the bull a heartfelt slap on the rump to urge him on. All at once catching sight of the cows awaiting him, Goliath suddenly forgot all about battle and trotted with ponderous majesty into the pasture, and Thierry let out a shaken laugh.

"Smooth as cream, eh?"

In the next moment he was surrounded by white-faced, anxious folk. Thierry hastily assured everybody that he wasn't hurt, rather amazing himself by his calmness. In a short time, he knew, he was probably going to be shaking like the proverbial leaf from reaction, but right now he seemed swathed in a blanket of tranquility, graciously accepting Simon's heartfelt words: "I am forever in your debt, my lord."

"Ah, Simon, I could hardly let Lisette be trampled."

But the old man continued to stare at him, eyes dark and shadowy. "In the time to come," Simon murmured in a voice suddenly deep with strength, "you will walk strange paths. Remember then that my blessing goes with you."

But then he blinked, as though surprised by his own words and, flushing, bowed and hurried away. Thierry glanced after the old man, feeling the faintest chill stealing through him. Feyness . . .

Ah, ridiculous. Simon was ancient enough to be entitled to a touch of strangeness, but Thierry had no such excuse. He waved off his cattleherd's shaken apologies—accidents did happen—and looked ruefully down at his dirt-covered, rumpled self. Most definitely time for a bath, and a change of clothing. Heigh-ho, maybe he could slip back into the manor before Gerard saw and—

"My lord!" said an indignant voice. "What *have* you been doing?"

Thierry glanced at the stocky, gray-haired, quietly elegant figure standing in the manor doorway and bit back a sigh.

"Playing with Goliath," he said, and received the expected blank stare. Gerard, Foretterre's steward, was an honest, competent man, efficient and genuinely kindhearted, but no one could ever have accused him of levity. "Never mind." He could feel himself starting to shake; sure enough, reaction to his narrow escape was setting in. "What is it, Master Gerard?"

"You promised we'd go over the estate's records today."

It was the last thing he wanted to do right now. But a vow was a vow, and Thierry held up a hand in resignation. "Let me clean myself up a bit, and then I'll surrender myself into your keeping."

Outside, the world was still wild and sweet with spring, full of birdsong. Within the long, narrow manor hall, all was quiet propriety. One of the newer sections of the manor, replacing the cold stone Great Hall of a hundred years ago, its walls were paneled in spotless, gleaming wood still smelling faintly of this morning's polish and broken only by the large fireplace of elaborately carved white stone. The hall was fashionably bare of furnishings save for a few chairs and narrow tables lining those walls, and an ornate canopied chair standing in solitary splendor at the hall's far end. Bars of sunlight filtered in through the tall, narrow windows, turning the wooden walls to gleaming amber and hitting the chair's occupant square in the face.

Thierry, freshly bathed and groomed in brocaded tunic and silken hose more befitting a count, twisted about as best he could to avoid the glare, struggling to keep a look of intent interest on his face as Gerard, standing tirelessly before him, droned on and on. It had been a long morning, and even after that bath, which had soaked most of the shock out of him, muscles strained by his dance with Goliath were beginning to complain. Thierry subtly twisted again, struggling not to wince, too polite to hurt Gerard's feelings by showing open boredom. But God, the wonderful smell of spring! He wished he was back outside, wandering in the green wonder of the forest, or even just on his knees again in the garden, discussing weeds with old Simon.

Ah, Gerard.

How could he be angry at the man? The steward had been almost a second father to him and kept Foretterre running well during all the years of the count's minority.

But you never do let a single point go by unnoted, do you?

". . . and so," Gerard continued methodically, unaware of his count's discomfort, "to date there are ten healthy new lambs, seven of them ewes, three calves—one heifer, two bull calves—"

"And the spring planting is going as it should," Thierry cut in. "Yes, I know. I was just out there checking everything myself."

"Uh . . . yes."

"Why, Master Gerard!" the count teased. "You don't approve, do you?"

"It's not for me to approve or disapprove, my lord."

"But a nobleman really shouldn't soil his hands with earth, or wander in fields and forest like a commoner, eh?"

Gerard's silence said volumes. Suddenly guilty, Thierry sighed. "I'm sorry I'm such a disappointment to you."

The steward stared at him in shock. "Don't even think such a thing! You are a kind, good, intelligent young man, and I—I'm proud of you. I thought you knew that. It's just . . ."

"That I'm never going to be the proper proud noble you want me to be."

"Oh, I didn't mean—"

"Never mind." Thierry gingerly stretched his stiff muscles. "We both know the estate is going well, God be praised. Now, have you any new business to discuss?"

"Ah, well, there is one thing. . . ."

That suddenly wary stance could only mean one thing. "You're going to bring up marriage again, aren't you?"

"Is there anything so wrong in that?" Gerard's dark eyes were suddenly very gentle. "It's not such a terrible thing.

I—Don't you think I still miss my Adele, even after all these years?"

"I'm sorry. I didn't mean . . ."

"It's all right. Adele is safe in Heaven. And even though the Lord never saw fit to give us a child of our own, I've had the joy of watching you grow up. Nothing would give me greater pleasure than to watch *your* son grow." Embarrassed, the steward hesitated, then added in a rush, "My lord, I know you're still a young man, but you *are* the last of your line. If that bull had—If the men hadn't—" Gerard shuddered, signing himself. "Praise the Lord you weren't hurt. But, to be quite selfish about it, if something happens to you, what becomes of the rest of us? You hold fealty to the king himself, not to some intermediary—"

"I've often wondered how Great-grandfather managed that."

"—and as a result, Foretterre would become Crown property, and we, why, whether or not we even continued to have a roof over our heads would depend on whatever stranger good King Charles picked to rule us. My lord, please. You really must begin thinking seriously about a wife, an heir."

Thierry bit back the urge to remind Gerard that Foretterre was so isolated it might be years before news of his death reached the king. "I know," he muttered. "I have thought. I went all the way to Paris last summer, remember? To pay my courtesies to our good king and his court?"

What a disaster *that* had been! Paris had seemed one overwhelming mass of close-packed buildings, the royal court a mass of close-packed folk like so many overdressed and smelly dolls . . . highborn dolls, with the gem-encrusted king on his throne the most unreal of them all, laughing at this awkward country boy who dared claim noble rank. . . . Thierry winced.

"If I couldn't find a suitable lady among all that glittering lot—"

"You weren't looking very hard," Gerard said sternly, and the count flushed.

"Could you picture any court lady happy in our little backcountry realm?" *Or, for that matter, being able to love the wildwood as I do?* No, he wasn't going to say *that* to Gerard.

But for a moment Thierry couldn't help but wonder. . . . What might it be like to be in love? He could almost see himself and . . . and some fair unknown wandering hand in hand through the forest, he feeding her berries not half as sweet as her lips (he reddened at the thought), showing her where the ferns formed a dark green tapestry unfurling down the hillside, or where flowers burst from shadow like so many stars, or that one spot where the stream turned to silver as it tumbled down the rocks. . . .

Ridiculous. "Bah," he said with forced humor, "a court lady would probably run screaming back to Paris the first time she saw a cow! 'Ooh, a monster! A monster!' "

That made Gerard smile in spite of himself, and Thierry pressed his advantage. "I'll give marriage serious thought, I promise. Now, is there any *new* business to discuss?"

"No, but—"

"Good." The young count got to his feet, stretching again. "I thank you, Master Gerard."

"But my lord, wait! Where are you going?"

A sweet spring breeze was stealing into the hall. Thierry took a deep, appreciative breath and waved a vague hand. "Out," he said, and smiled.

His people whispered about this hill, Thierry knew, murmuring all manner of dire stories because his ancestors hadn't built their manor on it, but on the lower hill nearby, because it grew so mysteriously free of all but grass and the three slender birches on its crest.

No mystery about it. They didn't build up here because there's no ready source of water, while down there is a nice network of streams and wells.

There wasn't much mystery about the lack of vegetation, either; the hill, he'd discovered as a curious boy with a shovel, was an outcropping of chalk on which few things could grow save grass and these three stubborn birches that were so shallowly rooted Thierry expected to lose them with every storm.

Hoping that would never happen, he reached out a hand to stroke sleek bark. These lovely things were perhaps his favorites of all the trees on his estate.

From where he sprawled comfortably up here on the hill, heedless of his aristocratic clothing, Thierry could see his entire estate, manor, village, and fields bisected by a thin brown ribbon of road and set against a dark green background of forest. Nibbling on a blade of grass, he picked out the tiny, perfect flame from Bernard the smith's forge in the village itself and a bright cloud of gold that was the grain Jeanne the goosegirl was tossing at her hungry charges. The sheep in their pastures and the cows in theirs (yes, and old Goliath, too) seemed perfectly wrought miniatures brought magically to life, as did the folk working in the neat, narrow strips of fields. Everything looked totally efficient, so efficient that Thierry thought wryly that were he to disappear, life in Foretterre would probably go on very nicely without him.

Sorry, Thierry told them all, good Gerard in particular, *I never will be quite as . . . dull and stodgy as you'd like.*

That wasn't quite fair. They might think him quite eccentric, but they loved him. And he, well, he loved the unruly lot of them in return, the extended family, headed by Gerard, that was all he'd known since his father had died in a riding accident five years back and left the already motherless boy an orphan.

He raised himself on one elbow. From here, the manor house looked like a toy, a rambling mixture of heavy, nearly windowless stone towers from the bad old days of war and siege, and of light, airy halls (some of them even set with precious panes of glass) dating from these more modern days of peace.

Not, Thierry admitted, that his home had ever seen a siege, Lord be praised. Though the one good road did lead, eventually, all the way to Paris, the mass of forest had pretty much discouraged any would-be invaders.

Ah, yes, forest. There were days when he imagined going off to live in the woodland, at home there as he hadn't been at court. His people could accept his taking a personal interest in such plebeian things as sheep and cattle; after all, it *was* his land. But Thierry was very well aware they were all scandalized that the count of Foretterre could survive in the wilderness like a lowborn forester.

But of course he couldn't run away. Gerard had been quite right; Foretterre really did depend on him. Besides, he didn't really want to run. No, what he really wanted was . . . was what?

Thierry stared blankly up at the sky. He should be thoroughly content; it was foolish to be anything else. And yet . . . lately there had been times when he was so lonely (ridiculous, amid all the bustle!) he could weep, and other times when he *knew* something was waiting for him, something so perilous and wonderful he could barely keep still for excitement.

What's wrong with me? What do *I want?*

A lady? A—a wife? Thierry groaned, thinking of the royal court and all that noise and stench and crowding, all those overproud, overpainted ladies, full of gossip and pettiness. God help him, he could never share his life with someone like that!

A peasant had no such problems. Give him enough land and crops on that land so he had time enough to think, and a peasant could afford to happily follow his heart. But nobles must always be cautious, must think in terms of political alliances, strategic advances. The last thing the count of Foretterre should want was something as . . . common, as unfashionable, as love.

Thierry said something short and sharp under his breath. What *was* the matter with him? He'd never been one for mooning over poet's words or tales of the old Court of Love; overseeing the shearing of sheep or the curing of hams hadn't left much room for romance. And he had no intention of going all soft and messy now!

When Thierry had first climbed up here, the air had been still, the birches' tender leaves hanging limp. But now their slender branches stirred softly, rustling in the rising breeze. Thierry's gaze sharpened. The day that had been so clear this morning was rapidly changing. Masses of ominously dark clouds were sweeping in from the west, and there was a sudden sharpness to the air. Fortunately most of the planting was already done, because if a storm wasn't on its way, he'd be very surprised.

Time enough for foolishness when he was safely off this exposed hill. Thierry got to his feet, shaking off bits of grass, and hurried back down for home.

THREE

Predator

The storm refused to break. It hung threateningly overhead all day, a brooding mass of clouds turning what light there was to an eerie dark green, and causing the confused birds to twitter and settle down for this unnatural night. The air grew still once more, so thick and heavy Thierry could have sworn it was pushing down on his head.

Storm, curse you! Storm, and get it over with!

Out in his pasture, Goliath pawed the ground ceaselessly, menacing birds and butterflies and his own harem, while in the manor house servants bickered with each other over the proper mopping of a floor or the folding of table linen. Dinner at Foretterre was usually a friendly, informal affair, count and commons eating in the same room if not at the same table, but with the storm looming overhead, food and conversation both quickly lost their savor. By nightfall, Thierry, having picked at his food and snapped at his servants till he was sick of himself, was very glad to give up and go to bed.

Earlier counts, living in days of perpetual wariness, had slept in small, narrow, easily defended cells. Dank, airless cells, Thierry thought with a shiver of distaste. The first thing he'd done as count was move here, to the newest wing, to this large, airy room with a true, large window overlooking the hill with his three pet birch trees. The window provided plenty of light, though he had to admit it made the room bitterly cold in the winter, even with the shutters closed and the fireplace (another radically new idea, a fireplace in a bedchamber) doing its best, and a heated brick warming the sheets of the massive curtained featherbed. Glass wasn't the answer. Glassblowers had yet to figure out a way to create panes larger than a man's hand, and even the finest of those panes—fragile, expensive things—had so many distortions in them they eliminated any view.

Besides, glass wouldn't keep out the chill and damp when there was a storm waiting to strike. Thierry let his manservants fuss over him for a time, then chased them away in sudden impatience and settled into bed, snuggling down gladly into the warmth of the thick feather mattress. Ah, this was better . . . he could feel the tension sliding away from him . . . sliding, sliding. . . .

The first incredible flash of lightning brought him bolt upright, realizing too late that no one had closed the shutters. As thunder echoed through the room, Thierry groaned, falling back to bury his head in the pillows. But he couldn't breathe that way, and as soon as he turned over, a second dazzling flash blazed across his closed eyes. He winced, reluctant to leave his nice, warm burrow. But he wasn't about to shout out for servants like some little boy afraid of thunder, so Thierry stumbled, barefoot and shivering, across the cold stone floor to lock the shutters himself.

He reached them just in time to see a white-hot bolt lance down from the clouds to strike one of his three pet birches, splitting it cleanly in two.

"Ah, no . . ."

But a new flash gave him a tantalizing hint of—what? Thierry froze, hands clamped on the windowframe, waiting tensely for the next bolt. There! A figure was huddled near the base of the broken tree. Dear God, some traveler must have foolishly camped under the birches and been struck by lightning!

Thierry didn't dare wait. Whoever was out there needed help at once. Pulling on the first clothes that came to hand, the count shouted for his servants.

No answer.

Hastily belting his sword about his waist—he wasn't going to rush blindly out into the night without a weapon—the count flung the door open, and was met by a wall of dense, heavy silence.

Impossible! They can't all *be asleep, not with all that noise!*

Yet so they were, and he—he couldn't wait. Even though a small inner voice was warning that something was very wrong here, that he should shake or slap someone else awake, Thierry found himself outside before he knew it, in the middle of a fantastic display of lightning. He gasped as a cold wind struck him, and wrapped the heavy wool of his cloak tightly about himself. Head down, he staggered his way up the hill. Odd, there wasn't any rain, nothing but wind and noise and blazes of light, and his inner voice was beginning to scream that this was never a natural storm, never. . . .

But he'd reached the crest of the hill, the bitter tang of the burnt, broken tree sharp in his nostrils. The figure still huddled at the birch's base. By the light of the dazzling flashes, Thierry realized with a shock of surprise that it wasn't a man at all, but a woman, slender and young, unbound hair streaming in a pale flood about her.

Now, what is she *doing here?*

Even peasant women never traveled alone. And this certainly wasn't a peasant, not in that silky, presumably costly, green gown: hardly traveling clothes!

"My lady," Thierry asked tentatively, "are—are you hurt?"

She didn't seem to hear or see him. Thierry reached out a wary hand to touch her shoulder—

A shriek of pure fury tore the air. For a brief, ridiculous second he thought she'd screamed. Then Thierry whirled, sword drawn, and saw a great black something plummeting down out of the clouds—an eagle, by the Lord, far larger than any eagle should be, eyes blazing as fiercely as the lightning, cruel beak agape, outstretched talons glinting like so many curving knives.

Buffeted by the wind from the vast wings, Thierry swung his sword two-handed as if it were one of his ancestors' broadswords, but the eagle sideslipped in the air with an angry cry. The edge of one wing struck Thierry a glancing blow, sending him sprawling, sword flying from his hand. The eagle cried out again, the sound this time for all the world like a savage laugh, and swooped, talons reaching for him. The count struggled to his feet, only to be knocked aside once more by a great ebon wing as the eagle swerved from the kill at the last moment.

The thing's playing with me!

But as the eagle dove yet again, Thierry saw its eyes blaze up blue-white with fury, never the eyes of anything natural (as if he'd ever had any doubt!) and realized it had abandoned games. As it plunged at him, this time after his life, the count didn't even try to regain his feet. Instead, he scrambled frantically for his sword, outstretched fingers touching, closing over the hilt. Twisting about, Thierry managed to get one knee under him, and lunged up blindly with all his might. He saw the blade pierce the eagle's breast—but it hit nothing but air. Thierry went sprawling forward onto his face. The wind rushed wildly about him for an instant, then a shriek that held a world of rage within it tore the night apart. Gasping, ears ringing, he glanced up.

The eagle was gone. The count scrambled to his feet, hardly believing what he saw, or didn't see.

"God, what was—sorcery? Illusion? Was I dreaming, or—"

He broke off abruptly, because the young woman had crumpled out of her rigid pose into a pathetic little heap, shivering convulsively.

"Ah, lady? . . . You . . . didn't have anything to do with . . . that, did you?"

No. Of course not. Besides, the eagle already seemed unreal, impossible, part of an eerie dream.

Thierry shook his head to clear it. Dream or not, the bruises forming where he'd hit the ground were real enough. He glanced about the too-silent night, feeling as though unseen eyes were watching, and shuddered. The whole matter could be cleared up once they were safely inside.

"Lady?"

When she still failed to react, he hesitated, wondering nervously if she, too, would vanish at his touch, then bent to wrap his cloak around her. No, she was warm and soft and real in his arms. The cloud of her hair held something of the sweet, spicy scent of the forest within it, and Thierry thought in one wild, confused rush of wonder that he could have stayed just as he was forever, crouched beside her on the hill, holding her.

Nonsense. He stood, pulling the woman gently to her feet. The storm had at last dissipated (or had it, he wondered with a new shiver of unease, been as sorcerous as the eagle, and as suddenly vanished?) and the air was cool and calm. The clouds were beginning to disperse, and Thierry's breath caught in his throat as a wary ray of moonlight picked out the woman's features in silver. Beautiful, oh, she was beautiful as a wild thing, with those sharp, proud features, those slanted eyes so brilliantly green. . . .

"Who are you?" he breathed. "How did you get up here?"

But she still showed no sign of being aware of him, and Thierry realized belatedly that even if the lightning hadn't actually burned her, she could hardly be in anything but complete shock. Below them, the manor house had come alive with flickering candlelight.

Finally! Thierry thought with weary humor.

The vagrant moonlight picked out the way back down the hill in pale silver. Thierry put a protective arm about the woman's slender, trembling shoulders, and they went slowly down the hill together.

➢

The stranger looked far less mysterious seen by homey firelight. Far younger, too. Thierry realized with a little shock that she was somewhere about his own age, or perhaps even a bit less. Settled in a chair in one of the guest chambers, wrapped in a blanket that hid her slim form and wild fall of hair, a goblet of mulled wine pushed into her hand by plump, motherly Suzanne, the count's housekeeper, she could almost have been mistaken for some perfectly ordinary girl of the village—save for the proud, foreign lines of that thin face, and those blank, unseeing eyes.

Ah, and she was still lovely in her own sharp-edged way, so lovely that his heart pounded at the sight, so lovely and fierce and lost, like a wild thing caught in a trap.

Like a wild thing saved from a black-winged predator that might or might not have been real. . . .

Who is *she? What was she doing out there? And what, in God's name, happened out there?*

"We haven't been able to get a word out of her, my lord," Suzanne whispered. "She doesn't seem to have been hurt by the lightning, but . . . well . . ." The woman touched a meaningful finger to her head. "It's possible she's not quite . . . right."

This wild, beautiful creature nothing more than a fool? Thierry refused even to consider it. But when he knelt by her side, the slanted green eyes remained blank as two panes of opaque glass, and he winced.

"Can you hear me?" he murmured. "Do you know where you are?"

Not a quiver of emotion stirred the thin, lovely face, and Thierry cried out in sudden pain. "Oh, please, say something. Nod at me, or—or—here, touch my hand."

"We've tried everything, my lord," Suzanne said sadly. "It's useless."

But Thierry could have sworn he felt the slightest pressure of cold fingers against his own. "You *can* hear me! I know you can. Listen to me: My name is Thierry. Do you understand? I'm Thierry, and—"

"My lord, please, she can't—"

"Thierry." It was the softest hint of sound.

"You *did* hear me, you *can* speak!"

"Yes." As though the speaking of his name had broken a spell, life flared into the green eyes. She stared into his face, gaze soft and wondering. "You . . . you are Thierry. . . ."

For a moment he couldn't seen to catch his breath. Staring into those warm green pools, he would have agreed if she'd called him Goliath. But all at once he came back to himself with a rush of joy. "Yes!" he exclaimed. "And you—you are . . ."

Long lashes dropped to veil the slanted eyes. "Glinfinial," she said after a long pause. "Call me Glinfinial."

And then, as though she could no longer hold off exhaustion, the girl sagged wearily back into the depths of the chair and slid into sleep.

FOUR

Mysteries . . .

"My lord?"

Thierry, who'd been standing aimlessly on the ramparts that topped the older part of the manor, staring blankly over his fields while his thoughts circled around and around the lovely, mysterious stranger, whirled at that soft voice.

Since there was no countess at Foretterre, the women had been hard put to come up with suitable noble clothing for the young woman, but Thierry thought that she somehow turned even the ill-fitting homespun gown into something rare and wonderful. Her pale hair, moonsilver touched with gold by the sunlight, was topped by a triangular cap curving down on either side to frame her face, emphasizing the high cheekbones and glowing green eyes, and Thierry said helplessly only, "Oh," and "Oh," again.

Idiot! Say something else! Be courteous to the lady!

But not a word would come.

"My lord? Is something wrong?"

"No, no, of course not. Uh . . . how do you feel?"

She smiled. "After sleeping for . . . how long was it? A day around? I feel most thoroughly rested!"

Her voice held the faintest hint of an accent, musical and strange as the Welsh he'd once heard a peddler speak. Yet it wasn't quite the sound of Welsh. . . .

"Has—has your memory returned?" he stammered. "D-do you remember what you were doing out there?"

Her glance fell. "I . . . can't tell."

"But surely you have family, friends?"

"I'm afraid I can't tell that, either." She glanced up at him, then down again. "My lord, I must thank you for your hospitality."

"Oh, please! I could hardly leave you out there in the storm!" Thierry struggled to say something further. But his thoughts seemed to be fluttering about like so many butterflies; he couldn't catch even one of them, and fell helplessly silent once more. For what seemed a long, wonderful while he could do nothing but simply stare at Glinfinial, who, to his awed delight, seemed to be just as fascinated by him.

"Uh, my lady . . ." he managed at last.

"Glinfinial, please."

"Lady Glinfinial. W-will you . . . will it please you to walk with me?" *Oh Lord, I* do *sound like an idiot!*

But Glinfinial only smiled. "My lord," she said, the faintest, most delicious of blushes coloring her fair skin, "it would indeed."

Simon bit back a grunt as he lowered himself to his knees in the manor garden. With age was supposed to come wisdom, but so far all he seemed to have gotten out of all his years was a back that complained if he moved too suddenly. Still, he thought with a slow smile, it was a small thing. And how could he complain on such a radiantly clear, blue-skied day? The sun was blissfully warm, and the combination of growing herbs and healthy earth smelled so rich it was almost intoxicating. And there was—

Something . . . Other.

A sprig of comfrey still caught in his hand, Simon straightened, *feeling* beyond any physical sense a sudden hint of strangeness. . . . He turned, wincing slightly, to see green, glowing green. . . .

Green eyes. A woman. A young woman, a girl, really,

looking warm and very normal, softly golden in the sunlight, her slanted eyes green. . . .

Her eyes. Almost without knowing it, Simon bowed to her, awestruck, barely aware of Count Thierry's polite introductions, instead heard himself saying, "I never thought to see one of your kind here, lady, not here in the sunlight."

"Simon!" Thierry exclaimed. "What *are* you saying? This is the Lady Glinfinial, not—not some night creature!"

"Didn't mean any harm by it." But Glinfinial's eyes were on him, greener than the grass, assuring him, plainer than words, *I mean no harm. Please, keep my secret.* And since That Kind never could lie, and since he didn't *feel* the slightest bit of wrongness to her, Simon found himself nodding to her in a conspiratorial fashion and adding, "Must have been the sun dazzling me. Forgive me."

But as he turned to the herbs once more, Simon's thoughts were wild with wonder.

"I hope old Simon didn't bother you." Thierry gave Glinfinial a worried glance. "He's . . . getting on a bit, and sometimes he says strange things. . . ."

"No harm done." Glinfinial leaned on a pasture fence as easily as any peasant girl. "That's a fine, sleek herd. Are all those cattle yours?"

"Most of them. The villagers own the rest, and—Glinfinial, who *are* you?"

She never flinched. "I told you, I don't—"

"You must remember *something!*"

"I . . . Now, who is *that* splendid fellow?"

Thierry gave the bull only a cursory glance. "That's Goliath. But you—"

"My lord, please." Glinfinial turned to look at him, green gaze steady. "When I can tell you everything, I shall, I promise."

"But . . ." Thierry let his voice trail away. How could he possibly tell her the truth: *I must know who you are, because—I think I'm falling in love with you!*

➢

Foretterre's little flock of children were making more noise this bright morning than usual. And there was a touch of wonder in their laughter that Thierry had never heard before. Curious, he strolled towards the hilarity—

And found Glinfinial in the midst of it all, playing tag with a dozen small boys and girls as easily as though she'd lived there far longer than a mere week or so, dancing lightly this way and that, never quite within reach of the plump, grubby little hands, graceful as a reed in the wind. Her hair had come loose from its confining cap, her sleeves were caught up almost to the shoulder, and there was a definite streak of mud on her skirt.

And Thierry's heart nearly stopped at the wonder of her.

Suddenly aware of him, Glinfinial stopped short, face flushed with excitement. For a moment her green eyes were quite unreadable. But then she gave an embarrassed little laugh, just like any other young woman, and brushed the wild hair back from her face. "I must look ridiculous!"

Wordless, he shook his head. Glinfinial shooed away the children and moved to his side, readjusting her clothing, still chuckling. "Ladies aren't supposed to act so indecorously, are they?"

"I . . . uh . . ."

"I hope I haven't done anything too scandalous. But I haven't had a chance to laugh like that, or just be silly in . . . I don't know how long! My father would have been mortified if he'd seen—" She broke off sharply, all laughter gone.

"Go on!" Thierry prodded. "What else do you remember?"

Glinfinial shook her head and walked hastily on. Thierry hurried after her, struggling to reassure her. "Don't be afraid, it will all come back, truly it will. And in the meanwhile, well, I . . . uh . . ." *I what?* he thought frantically. "I thought maybe you'd like to see more of my lands."

She moved beside him like a silent shadow, so clearly wrapped up in her own unhappy thoughts that Thierry wasn't sure what else to do or say. What *did* one say to someone who'd lost everything but her name?

But as they entered the first stand of forest, Glinfinial's dark mood suddenly turned back to sunlight. With a mischievous little laugh, she darted ahead, disappearing into the underbrush without so much as a rustle. Thierry stood alone, abandoned.

"Glinfinial?" he called warily. "My lady, where are you?"

For one eerie moment, hearing the normal stirrings of the forest starting up again as though nothing had disturbed them, he could almost believe she'd been nothing but illusion, like a ghostly woman out of one of old Simon's tales.

No, that's not true, she's real, of—of course she's real, she has *to be real—*

Thierry let out a startled yelp as something small and hard rapped him on the head. What—an acorn! Glancing up, he saw Glinfinial stretched out easily on a tree limb.

"How did you—"

She sprang lightly to the ground in a swirling of gown and hair. "I always *was* good at climbing trees, at least I can tell you that much." Her eyes sparkled with humor. "We were growing too somber for such a lovely day. And such a lovely forest!" Glinfinial inhaled deeply, head thrown back. "It smells so wonderfully *alive*, as though you could put a hand on a tree trunk and feel the life coursing inside."

Thierry grinned. "I thought I was the only one who felt that way."

"Hardly. How much of this is yours?"

"A fair portion. The rest is Crown land or just plain wilderness."

Glinfinial bent to touch a leaf. "Mint?"

"Yes. There's a whole patch of it a little further along. It's a pretty spot. Would you like to see it?" But then Thierry hesitated in sudden uncertainty. "Ah . . . if you don't mind being here, that is. I mean, with me, without an . . . attendant?"

"Without a chaperon, you mean?" Glinfinial asked, the

glint of mischief back in her eyes. "Oh, I don't think we need one. As the children would say, 'You can't catch me!' "

With that, she darted forward again, racing lightly down a winding deer path. Feeling the same delicious silliness that had seized her enfold him, Thierry hurried after her, snatching at her trailing sleeves. Off to their left, the land dropped sharply down into a gully; through his panting, he could hear the sound of rushing water at its bottom, and thought, *Better be careful, don't want to slip—*

The earth crumbled under his feet. With a startled yell, the count tumbled helplessly down, bruised by rocks and roots, ending up with a mighty splash in the middle of the stream.

"Thierry!" Glinfinial shrieked, scrambling down after him. "Are you hurt?"

He sat up, dripping, pulling reeds out of his hair, spitting out what felt like a whole mouthful of silt. Glinfinial's worried cries ended in a strangled gasp of laughter.

"S-sorry!" she exploded. "I—I can't help it, you look so—so—*elegant*!"

Thierry started to say something—he wasn't sure what—but just then a reed slid slowly and majestically down over his eyes, and he, too, erupted into laughter. With Glinfinial's help, he struggled out of the stream and collapsed on its bank, Glinfinial at his side, both of them still giggling helplessly.

"This—this is no good," the girl gasped at last. "You'll c-catch a chill."

"I know."

But as she turned to him, her face so close to his own, Thierry felt the laughter fade within him, and saw her face grow very serious as well. For one endless moment, something warm and awesome trembled in the air between them, and very cautiously Thierry leaned forward—

But Glinfinial scrambled up with a nervous little laugh. "This is silly. You need to get into dry clothing."

Thierry sighed. She was right, of course. This was hardly

the time or place for . . . well . . . for anything else. "Here I thought I knew every bit of this forest," he said ruefully, getting to his feet, wincing at the chilly touch of clammy cloth against his skin. "I'm not usually so clumsy."

Glinfinial's eyes glinted with humor. "Maybe a *lutin* pushed you."

"Ah, you know about those little creatures, too?"

"Oh, yes." Her voice was so serious that he couldn't tell if she was jesting or not. "They're such mischievous things, prank-playing forest sprites. Or," she added demurely, "so the stories tell."

"That's what old Simon told me, too." As they started back toward his estate, Thierry continued, trying to take his mind off his discomfort, "I used to listen to his tales all the time when I was growing up. He made it all sound so *real.* Ha, for all I know, he was telling me the truth! Maybe he visited with Other folk when he was a boy, and that's why he's so Otherly now himself."

Thierry meant it as a joke, but to his surprise, Glinfinial didn't even smile. "Anything's possible," she murmured.

"Ah. Well. At any rate, thanks to Simon, I know all about *lutins* and *galipotes* and all the rest of that supernatural lot. Useful knowledge for a count, eh?" he added with a laugh, then sneezed.

"Enough," Glinfinial said firmly. "Come, hurry. Dry clothes and a warm drink for you, my lord count!" Taking his arm, she virtually dragged him home.

Juliette, second underservant to the housekeeper Suzanne, plump and pert as any sparrow, stopped folding linen long enough to whisper, "Who do *you* think she is?"

Louise, first underservant, tall and narrow faced, crossed herself nervously, nearly dropping the tablecloth she held. "No one human, that's for sure, not with those cat-green eyes and that heathenish name."

"Oh, that's ridiculous! Of course she's human!"

Louise sniffed. "Maybe."

"Don't be silly, Louise! Remember, good Father Denis spoke with her, and if *he* didn't seem to be worried, it's hardly up to you to—"

"What about Goliath? I mean, that bull hates everyone—except her! He fawns on her like a calf!"

"Yes, but . . ."

"And what about her name? Glinfinial. Whoever heard a name like that? Heathenish, I say. Or," Louise added darkly, "maybe worse."

"I like her," murmured shy little Claire, third underservant, "she's nice."

The others laughed. "Nice!"

"Well, yes." Blushing fiercely at so much attention, Claire continued bravely, "She always smiles at me, and wishes me good day in that sweet voice of hers. Besides, remember when I fell and hurt my wrist and everybody thought it was broken? I was so scared and it hurt so much I started to cry."

"Oh, Claire," Louise muttered. "It couldn't have been broken, could it? You were using it freely afterwards."

"Yes, but that's because *she* held it, just for a moment, and murmured something over it—and the pain went away, I swear it!"

Louise and Juliette stared at each other in sudden alarm, but Claire never noticed. Shaking out a tablecloth, she continued cheerfully, "And his lordship seems quite smitten by her. Even if she's been here for nearly a fortnight and we *still* don't know who she really is."

"No one human," Louise said flatly, and this time no one argued with her.

Glinfinial stood alone at the window of the guest chamber, looking out into the first pale light of morning. Ah, how wondrous it all was, sunrises bright and fresh as new life, warm golden rays sparking new, daylight colors out of the earth. . . .

A flicker of motion caught her gaze. She looked down to where Thierry chatted with early-rising servants there in the courtyard, and her heart seemed to spring to life like the sun-touched earth. Maybe he lacked some of the tall, fine grace of her father's people. Maybe he lacked their cold, perfect beauty. But oh, he was fair! And wonderfully warm and kind of heart! Glinfinial thought back to the cool, quiet, unemotional folk who had been all she'd known till now, and could have sobbed aloud for the contrast.

Powers, Powers, what was she going to do? How much longer could she keep up this pretense? Old Simon, with his quirky human Gift, had already pretty much puzzled out what she was, though he'd sworn to keep silent. But if the others so much as guessed, as they already seemed to be doing . . .

Glinfinial turned away, rubbing an angry hand across suddenly wet eyes. It had been a mistake to speak to that monstrous bull in her father's tongue, particularly when people were about; she should have known the magic behind the simple words would have charmed the beast. And she never should have stopped to help that child, that shy little Claire. But the girl had been so frightened, and her pain had echoed through Glinfinial's own nerves till she'd done what she would have done with one of her father's kind, starting the injury to healing and drawing off the pain.

But there must be no more of this! She must *not* draw attention to herself. The servants were already shying from her ever so slightly, and she could have sworn she'd heard them whisper words like "witch," and "sorcery." Her father's warnings returned to her in force: "*These people are fools! Fools terrified of magic! And that terror can all too quickly turn to hate. Beware of them!*"

They thought anyone who was too different from their norm must be in league with evil. And the price for such a sin was the stake, the flames. . . . Glinfinial shivered at the thought, hugging her arms tightly about herself, her mind insisting on conjuring an image of herself bound and helpless, wood smoldering about her, the angry crowd lusting for her death, Thierry at their head—

No, ah, no, not Thierry! She couldn't bear the thought of hatred in *his* eyes!

Glinfinial turned back to the window, staring down at the young count till her eyes ached.

She would be human, only human. There would be no more mistakes. And whatever the cost, there would be no more magic!

FIVE

. . . And Revelations

"But you *can't* be in love with her." Gerard's voice was low and urgent. "Yes, I admit she's pretty and graceful as—as a dancer, and speaks with a definitely cultured tone." The steward paused thoughtfully. "She does seem an intelligent young woman, too."

"Indeed," Thierry murmured. "Those questions she asked you about the running of an estate had you perplexed, didn't they?"

"She was merely expressing polite interest," Gerard decided. "Her manners do speak of good breeding. And there must surely be noble blood in her veins if she speaks so well. Oh, but my lord Thierry! You don't know anything about her!"

"Save that she's pretty and graceful as a dancer," Thierry echoed drily. "And has a quick wit, a clever mind, and quite acceptable manners."

"Oh, please! You know very well what I mean. Remember who and what you are!"

"Could I ever forget?"

Gerard let out an impatient gust of a sigh. "Thierry, my lord, if you were some common lad, I'd say, 'Go, love your mystery lady, and be happy.' But you are *Count* Thierry, you *are Foretterre*, and you simply cannot permit yourself to love this—this stranger."

Thierry looked past Gerard to where Glinfinial strolled through the manor garden. Up to this point he'd always wondered at Simon's whim at planting purely ornamental flowers as well as more practical herbs, but now, seeing the girl framed against a bank of early roses, their earnest red making her seem a pale golden sprite out of legend, he blessed the old gardener. But there was more to Glinfinial than anything as easily defined as physical beauty, and after a moment's mental floundering, Thierry realized what it was: She bore with her a constant sense of wonder, as though everything she saw, down to the everyday marvel of sunlight, was something new and rare and precious.

"Cannot love her?" Thierry murmured, too softly for his steward to hear. "Too late for that, Gerard. I think I already do."

Old Simon's deft, gnarled hands neatly went about their work, there in the sunlit garden, nipping back new growth so this plant would grow more lushly, bracing a stem against a stake to strengthen that plant, but his mind was all on Glinfinial.

Amazing. No, no, more than amazing! True, he had always known there were Others in field and forest, even if he'd never seen more than the barest glimpse once of something that *might* have been wise, ancient, alien eyes staring at him from the forest: magical, nonhuman Others, mischievous *lutins* or perilous *galipotes*. No matter how good Father Denis might try to deny it, Simon knew magic existed. Didn't he himself have the smallest bit of the Sight, passed down through his family for untold ages?

The old man straightened with a small, wondering smile. Sight or no Sight, he had never thought to actually see, to speak with, to touch the hand of one of the High Ones, one such as the Lady Glinfinial.

She wasn't at all how he'd imagined one of Them to be. For all her mystery, the hint of Otherly peril, Glinfinial was as kind as any human maid, wise in the way of green growing things, and so lovely in her young, sharp-featured way that she roused a faint, bittersweet ache in his heart, making him remember his own, long-gone youth. It was easy to understand how Count Thierry could be so smitten by her. Simon glanced skyward, thinking he could only pray to Heaven that—

Tsk, look at that. Ivy had somehow insinuated itself onto the manor wall high over his head, right up under the slope of red-tiled roof.

And here I thought we'd gotten it all last year!

Ivy-covered walls might look pretty, but the tenacious roots sank deep into mortar, crumbling it, and eventually bringing down the whole wall.

Simon glanced around. One of the workmen had left a ladder lying in shadow, and he reached for it, then hesitated. He did, of course, have helpers; any vegetable garden big enough to feed a manor house was too big to be tended by only one man. Still . . . there wasn't anyone in sight now, and it was too warm a day for shouting. Besides, Simon thought with a sniff, if he *did* call for one of the brash young things, he'd have to put up with the sideways glances, the subtle smiles that said what had never been said aloud: *old man. Weak old man.*

"Weak," Simon muttered, wrestling with the ladder. "I may be old, but I am *not* weak!"

Placing the ladder firmly against the manor wall, he started up, too wise to think about what he was doing, how high he was climbing. A little more, just a little more . . . Curse it! Even standing on the ladder's top rung, he . . . couldn't . . . quite . . . reach the ivy. . . . But if he stretched up just a little higher . . . His hand closed about one glossy green strand, and he pulled. But the ivy clung stubbornly to the wall. Simon set his lips in an impatient line, hearing his mind insist, *weak old man.* Curse it, no! He gave one mighty tug on the ivy—

And overbalanced. Falling helplessly backwards, Simon

had time only for one anguished thought: *Not like this! This is a stupid way to die!*

Glinfinial still wasn't aware of him, and Thierry froze, surrounded by leaves, watching her in wonder. Oh, how lovely she was, even when all she did was raise an early rose so she could sniff it. But even now she seemed so somber, so remote.

How can she be otherwise? Losing her memory must be such a frightening thing!

And yet, for all the lingering hint of sadness in those green eyes, Thierry sensed a hidden joy about her, even a touch of mischief. If only he knew how to rouse that sleeping laughter, to see her happy and lovely as the roses—

"Ow!"

Thierry surged forward in alarm, but Glinfinial, finger to mouth, shook her head. "It's nothing. I only pricked myself. I didn't realize these roses had thorns—I—I mean, such sharp thorns."

He stared. "Don't they have roses where you come from?"

Glinfinial's glance was sharp with anguish. "I . . . I can't tell you," she gasped, and turned away sharply.

Thierry cried out, "I'm sorry, I didn't mean . . . oh, please, don't weep!"

He hadn't meant to do more than put a comforting hand on her arm. But somehow, he wasn't quite sure how, he found himself holding her instead, holding her closely, her hair like a sweet, soft cloak around them, and their faces were so close that their lips were almost touching. . . .

Glinfinial, with a nervous little laugh, pulled away. "I wasn't crying, really I wasn't."

"Glinfinial, I think I . . ."

But he couldn't say, *I love you.* He couldn't admit to this strange girl that he'd been shaken from his first sight of her, that she filled that aching, lonely little spot in his heart.

Who is she? his mind insisted. *What is she?* He'd heard the servants whisper about her, hinting at old beliefs, foolish superstitions. Bah, he wasn't an idiot, to be frightened of strangers!

But he *was* a count. Gerard, alas, was right. No matter how he felt, he must, before he dared love, know the truth about—

All at once Glinfinial cried out in shock, eyes wide and wild. She hastily waved Thierry to silence, head turning abruptly as though she were hunting. "There!" she gasped. "Oh, come, hurry!"

She darted forward like a deer, and the bewildered Thierry raced after her, rounding a corner of the mansion's wall to see—

"Simon!"

The old man lay with limbs splayed out, like a broken doll. Thierry threw himself down at Simon's side, not quite daring to touch him in case he did more damage. Though there didn't seem to be any broken bones, Simon lay frighteningly still. A ladder lay to one side; Simon must have fallen from it, maybe hit his head. The count looked wildly around for help, feeling helpless as a stupid child.

His gaze froze on Glinfinial. She was standing stock still, her pale face so rigidly blank it was almost . . . inhuman. And *Inhuman!* screamed his brain at the sight of those wide, opaque green eyes that seemed to drink in the light and gave nothing back. All at once he believed the servants' tales, and cried out, "Help him!"

That alien, rigid gaze fixed on Simon's face, she shook her head.

"Help him!"

"I . . . can't . . ."

"Glinfinial!" Thierry reached up and pulled her down beside him. "He'll *die* if you don't help him!" He caught her by the shoulders, aching to shake some life back into her. "You can help, I know it!" Before he could control himself, all the fears he'd struggled to ignore came tumbling out. "You talk with animals, and they understand you! You healed little

Claire's broken arm! I don't know who you are, what you are, but I know you can heal Simon!"

For a moment her stare, clear and blank as green ice, met his. Then all at once he read total, hopeless despair in those alien eyes. She sagged in his arms with a weary sob, as though something had given way within her, and murmured, "Yes."

Glinfinial studied Simon a long, long while, as though somehow *feeling* for injuries. At last she sighed and took the old man's head very gently between her hands.

"The damage is here," she murmured. "His skull is fractured."

"You c-can help him?"

"Oh, Thierry, I don't know. I've never tried something like this before. It's not beyond healing, I've seen my father's people heal worse. B-but I may not have the strength alone. Will you help me?"

"Of course!" *Even though I haven't the vaguest idea what you're talking about.* "What should I do?"

"Grant me your strength when I need it. No, don't ask questions. You'll understand when the time comes."

She bent over Simon. And then . . . Thierry could hardly have said what happened then. A warmth, a mist, stole over the three of them, an eerie, swirling Otherwhen, as though they were suddenly alone in a place apart from the world. Thierry gasped, all at once realizing that he *felt* Simon's injury like a wrongness itching at his mind, *felt* Power surging from Glinfinial to heal that wrongness, knew without knowing that her strength was failing, and took her hand in his, mingling strength with strength as the wrongness faded, and the mistiness faded, and—

They were back in reality, Simon groaning and stirring. The old man's eyes opened, and he slowly sat up. "My lord? That . . . was quite a fall I took." He ran wary hands over himself, and laughed in wonder. "Could have sworn . . . I never thought to get out of it with . . . ow! . . . nothing worse than bruises."

Thierry, all at once as weary as though he'd run all the way to Paris, managed a shaken smile. "You—you were lucky," he said, giddy at the understatement.

But what *had* happened? Could Glinfinial and he somehow, bewilderingly, actually have worked . . . magic together?

Simon seemed to think so. Eyes wide with reverence, he murmured, "It was *your* doing, lady, wasn't it?"

But Glinfinial didn't answer. She and Thierry stared at each other, shaking with exhaustion.

"I think we must talk, lady," Thierry said at last.

"So be it," she murmured in resignation.

They sat alone together in a deep, softly cushioned window seat, away from prying servants. "First you must promise not to interrupt," Glinfinial began warily.

"And you must promise to tell me the truth."

"My lord, I never lie." Her smile was wan. "None of my father's people do."

"Your father's people?"

"The Faerie folk. Ah, wait, you promised not to interrupt! Listen. My father is Tiernathal, Faerie Lord of—of a small domain hidden deep within the forest. Moonlight makes him restless, and he often wanders into mortal wilderness. And that's where he met my mother. She . . . was human, a young woman named Adele who was fleeing marriage to a cruel, cold man. When she found herself facing a tall, golden Lord of Faerie, one who spoke gentle, tender words to her . . ." Glinfinial sighed. "I doubt my father needed any spells to enchant her. He stole her away to his Realm that night, heedless of what any of his people might say or think. Even his wife.

"And there, some few years later, his human lady bore the Faerie Lord a daughter."

"You? . . ."

"I thought you weren't going to interrupt."

"Sorry. Please, go on."

"Among my father's people, it's the custom to name a newborn child after whatever the mother first sees. In my case, it was the play of moonlit leaves in the wind. And so I am Glinfinial, Wind-in-Leaves in your language, Windleaf." She hesitated. "That was the only gift my poor mother gave me, other than life itself. She died soon after my birth. I was raised by my father's people, together with the two daughters of his wife."

"Ah."

"Oh, don't give me that pitying look! I wasn't treated harshly, even by her. Children are rare among the Faerie folk, and cherished." She chuckled. "In fact, my father is considered something of a wonder for having sired no less than three children!"

But Thierry saw the faint shadow in her eyes, and murmured, "Still, his wife could hardly have loved you."

"She didn't," Glinfinial admitted, a touch too lightly. "But then, I couldn't have been the lovable child, either, half one thing, half another, never quite knowing where my true heart lay." She added reluctantly, "I think my father resented me. For my human blood. For reminding him of his own weakness."

"I hardly find loving a human a weakness!"

"But you're not Tiernathal, proud Faerie Lord!" She shook her head. "At any rate, I inherited my father's restlessness, and often wandered out of my father's twilight Realm into mortal lands." Glinfinial smiled, remembering. "There I found delight in the warm, living forest. There I saw the sun for the first time, its light filtering down through the leaves like so much fairy gold, and realized my mother's blood gave me immunity to its rays.

"And there I saw a true human for the first time, a young man who loved the forest as much as I. And I . . . lost my heart to him."

"Ah." It was a smothered little cry of pain. She loved another! "D-did you tell him how you felt?"

Her gaze dropped. "No. I didn't quite dare."

"But—"

"It doesn't matter now. What I didn't know while I was spying on my young man, and wishing I had the courage to approach him, was that my half sisters, Tareniel and Serenial, were spying on *me*. They went flying right back to our father with the news. And he—oh, he was furious at all three of us! Me, for my—my treachery. They, for their tattling. He bespelled all three of us for punishment, encased us, body and mind, in the three birch trees that stand—used to stand—out there."

"*My* trees?" Thierry squawked. "I never guessed—"

"How could you? But there we were, trapped in our tedious prisons till the day we should repent. And *that*, I swore, I should never do."

"Then what broke the spell?"

"You. Every time you went up there, your human touch weakened the magic. And you bore iron." She shuddered delicately. "Iron doesn't hurt me; my mother's blood protects me. But oh, how that most Earthly metal hates Faerie magic! On the night of that storm, the last of the spell tore apart, and my sisters and I were free. They fled back to my father's Realm, but I refused to go with them."

"Good God," Thierry exclaimed, remembering that savage night. "That great black eagle was real, wasn't it? It was your father's sending!"

Glinfinial nodded. "I could feel how furious he was at you; his rage was like a great dark weight crushing me so I couldn't even think clearly. But your iron sword shattered the sending before he could hurt you, Powers be thanked. And now I'm here. You d-don't . . . hate me, do you? For being what I am?"

"Hate you! Dear Lord, no! But why didn't you tell me the truth from the start? Why pretend—"

"I was afraid. All the time I was growing up, my father told me again and again how humans fear magic, how they hate it, how they—how they destroy what they hate."

"Your father *hates* humans!" Thierry protested. "You can't

believe anything he says about us!" But then he paused. "Glinfinial, we can hardly keep all this a secret."

"I know."

"For the sake of my people—and since Father Denis is certainly going to ask the same thing—I do have to ask this: What magics can you work?"

"Nothing of Darkness, I swear it! I won't harm you or your people, my word on it. Besides," she added with a touch of rueful humor, "you saw about the strongest magic I can wield when we healed Simon. My powers aren't even half those of someone wholly of Faerie."

Of Faerie. Ageless Faerie. Thierry, feeling his cheeks reddening, stammered out, "And . . . uh . . . how . . . old are you?"

She laughed outright. "What do you expect? That I'm two or three hundred? No. As far as I can guess—the time in my father's Realm isn't exactly the same as mortal time—I have sixteen or seventeen years."

Why should he be relieved? Why should it matter, when he knew she loved someone else? Thierry didn't want to say it, but say it he knew he must. "What of your human young man? Does he know you're free?"

To his surprise, Glinfinial chuckled. "He does indeed."

"Where is he?" Although he'd rather have been stricken mute than continue, Thierry added bravely, "I will take you to him."

"Oh, Thierry!" Now she was laughing anew. "Don't you see?"

"See what? What's so funny?"

"That young man, my kind, wonderful, naive dear—is you!"

Dark Moonlight

Surely, Thierry thought giddily, there had never been so bright or warm or golden a springtime. Surely life itself had never been so golden!

She loves me, she does, she loves me! He was never going to tire of repeating that marvel. *She does love me!*

Once, Thierry admitted to himself, he'd laughed at minstrels' tales of romance, calling them silly tales that couldn't possibly come true. Now he could have laughed at himself instead, because he loved Glinfinial just as fiercely as any of those fairy tale heroes had loved their ladies—more, because she wasn't some flower-frail princess, but a real, warm, wonderful young woman who could act the perfect lady if she chose, yet thought nothing of climbing a tree if the whim struck her!

Thierry knew his people were still all agog over what had happened, over Simon's healing and the stranger having turned out to be both of incredible origin and of very noble blood indeed (though none of them could quite decide if a Faerie Lord was equal to a duke, or prince, or—most deliciously alarming—king). But Glinfinial had been wrong to be afraid; there were enough believers in old ways and older magics among the people of Foretterre for them to accept her. Particularly since she'd proved to them that neither sunlight nor Father Denis's holy relics could hurt her. There was nothing to fear, for them, for her, for anyone!

And yet, whispered his mind, *and yet . . .*

For all the sunlit joy, something was ever so subtly wrong. With every day that passed, Thierry could have sworn he saw a growing shadow darkening Glinfinial's eyes. And he thought he knew the cause.

"Glinfinial, forgive me. I should have realized this earlier, but it has to be so frightening for you. You've left behind everything you knew, family, customs, friends."

She only shrugged, a little too casually to be believable. "Let's just say I couldn't be happy with twilight now that I've known sunlight."

"Ah, yes. But I'll try to make it up to you," Thierry continued urgently. "As much as I can, I mean. Foretterre can be your home for as long as you wish it."

"And you, Thierry? What do *you* wish?"

"That—that you never want to leave," he stammered. "That you stay here with me as . . . as . . ." Oh, why wouldn't the words come smoothly? "Glinfinial, what I'm trying to say is, we've known each other for only a very short while, and I'm aware there are differences between us—"

"You're a boy and I'm a girl," she teased.

"Please! I'm trying to tell you I—I love you!"

"I know that, dear heart."

"And I—Glinfinial, a count *must* be wed, but here I've been delaying, making excuses, sure there was someone just out of reach who . . . But she's not out of reach anymore and I—you—I—" *Curse it all, I sound like an idiot!* "What I'm trying to ask you is if you will be—"

"No . . ."

To his amazement, he saw her eyes fill with tears. She turned away quickly. "I can't marry you. I d-don't dare."

"Whyever not? Look you, if you're worried about—about race, or rank or religion—I don't care! My *people* don't care! Even Father Denis doesn't really care, not once you proved you could enter his chapel and—"

"Thierry, please. That's not it. My father . . ."

"Oh, *him!* He doesn't dare leave his shadowy Realm. You're free of him, love."

"No."

"Yes! He hasn't done a thing since he sent that eagle thing, has he?"

"No, but—"

"You see? He knows I carry iron. Ha, everyone in Foretterre carries *some* iron! Besides, he can't act in sunlight, I know that much, and—"

"There's still the night. Oh, my dear Thierry, I haven't escaped him, not really. I'm still bound to him by blood, the strongest tie of all, blood and magic. He's not going to leave us alone, love. He'll never let me be human. Oh, no, my father is simply biding his time." She was trembling so strongly that Thierry ached to comfort her, but Glinfinial turned away before he could touch her, hugging her arms tightly about herself. "He's going to drag me back to him," she murmured, eyes bleak. "And there's nothing either one of us can do to stop him."

Thierry lay alone in his bed, feeling further from sleep than he ever had in his life, thinking over what Glinfinial had said. No matter how terrified she might be of her father—and he sounded like a grim, bitter man indeed—the count just couldn't convince himself that they were in any danger. But, he admitted wryly, he couldn't exactly be at ease, either.

At last Thierry sighed and raised a hand to the love token about his neck, a small silver moon suspended from a delicate silver chain. Glinfinial had given it to him, just as he'd given her a golden brooch in the shape of an oak leaf (what better gift to someone named Windleaf?) that had once belonged to his mother.

Glinfinial had been very moved by the exchange of gifts. No, come to think of it, that had been more than mere emotion. It had been something almost magical. . . .

"These gifts will keep us together, love," she had said, her Fa-

erie eyes wide and mysterious. *"Come what may, these gifts will always keep us together."*

More than that she had refused to explain.

Thierry shrugged, smiling to himself. Life with a half Faerie would never be uncomplicated. "So be it," he murmured in acceptance, and closed his eyes. He still wasn't sleepy, but at least he could relax . . . relax and . . .

"So. This *is the one my daughter has chosen, this weak little fool of a human."*

Thierry frowned, knowing he was asleep, knowing he must be dreaming. And yet the words continued in his mind with undreamlike crispness, as clear as though someone spoke them aloud.

"Do you think to keep her, little human? Do you think you can match yourself against me?"

And all at once the dreaming Thierry saw a tall, lean figure cloaked in robes that glinted cold silver. Silver hair framed a pale, sharp, elegant face, and Thierry winced to see in that coldness a sharp, fierce, bitter echo of Glinfinial's face. But there was never any trace of human warmth here, never any trace of human pity. This could only be Glinfinial's father, Tiernathal the Faerie Lord. Eyes terrible with the weight of Power stared at Thierry till, to his disgust, he heard himself whimper like a child in his sleep, and struggled in vain to wake.

"I will take my daughter back tomorrow night, human." Tiernathal's voice was sharp with scorn. *"Tomorrow night. And you, poor, weak, magicless thing, will be unable to stop me."* The Faerie Lord paused a thoughtful moment. Then, eyes like cold, hating flame, he continued softly, *"A warning, human: Do not try to fight me. For if you do, I promise you pain, I promise you grief, I promise you death."*

"I'm not afraid!" Thierry gasped out—

And awoke, sick with shock, heart racing, body shaking with an inner chill. Dear God, dear God, that had never been only a dream. No, no, he'd seen Tiernathal, he'd seen Glinfinial's father, and heard his warning.

"You will not win," Thierry whispered to the Faerie Lord. "Wherever you are, I promise you *this*: You will not win!"

Of course. He was going to challenge the magic of Faerie, without a single spell to his name.

"But I have sunlight," Thierry murmured. "I have cold iron. And oh, I have Glinfinial's love!"

The next night, the fatal night, Thierry ringed Glinfinial round with iron in her bedchamber, his guards encircling them both in a thicket of outward-pointing spears. The cool silver light of the rising moon slid in through the room's narrow window, glinting off the iron spearheads, slipping coldly down the blade of Thierry's drawn sword.

"Now, love," he murmured to her, "let's see your father find his way through all this!"

"Don't boast." Glinfinial's eyes were shut, her face pale with strain. "Thierry, please. I hear my father calling to me, I *feel* him pulling at me. . . . And the night has so far to run."

Thierry started to reassure her, but his tongue seemed all at once too thick for speech. The night was growing so warm, the air so soft. . . . He heard one of the guards yawn, then another, and tried to snap out, "Stop that!" But the air was too heavy, the words wouldn't come, he was swaying on his feet, and far, far away someone was playing a harp, the melody so soothing it caressed the ear, coaxed the brain to forget, forget . . . and he could only listen . . . listen. . . .

"No—" gasped Thierry. His sword seemed heavier than stone, but he dragged it up with both hands, resting his forehead against the flat of the blade. And for a moment the touch of iron cleared his mind as he'd hoped. But in that moment, the count knew how foolish he'd been to think he could so easily have kept Glinfinial safe. The Faerie Lord had no need to risk himself against iron! No, all Tiernathal needed to do was what he was doing: placing sleep upon them from afar.

But it was difficult to think, even with iron's aid. As the soft, soft music continued, Thierry's arms grew so weary, the sword was so heavy. . . . With a cry of despair, he let it fall. All around him, the guards were settling wearily to the floor, and he . . . he ached to follow them. . . .

"No . . . I won't. . . ."

"But . . . his mind refused to think, his body refused to stand. . . .

"I can't . . . Glinfinial . . ."

He heard her stifled sob. He felt her long, silky hair brush against his arm, as though she were slowly being pulled away from him. Thierry made one last, valiant effort to move, but his legs refused to obey him. Helplessly, he sank into magic-laden sleep.

"*Hear me, human.*" It was Tiernathal's voice. "*Heed me well. Were it left to me alone, you would die here and now for your presumption. But by the Laws of Magic, I must give you this one chance. Go after Glinfinial alone, seek her out and never falter, and perhaps you will live long enough to win her back.*"

With that, the sleep spell dissolved. Thierry scrambled to his feet in the midst of swearing, frightened guards, and glanced frantically about.

Glinfinial was gone.

Tiernathal stared at his fierce-eyed, defiant daughter facing him like a hot-willed, wild thing there in his private audience chamber. Most of his subjects would have been subdued by the sheer quiet, the tranquility of that room with its simple wooden benches, its smooth, unmarked marble walls. But she was very much his daughter, for all her shameful blood, and mingled fear and rage blazed out from her in undiminished fury.

"Did you really think I would let you stay in *their* world?" he asked. "Did you really think I would let you soil yourself with a human?"

"Why not?" she snapped. "You did!"

Tiernathal was shocked at the sudden savage urge he felt to strike out at her. *Like a human, just like a brutish little human. No! Control. Control.* He straightened slowly, face a careful mask. "Be still, Glinfinial." The words were edged with delicate warning. "You may be my daughter, but you are also my subject. You shall not challenge me again."

"Father, this is ridiculous! You don't want me because I'm half human, we both know that's the truth. Then let me go! Let me live my own life!"

"Among the . . . animals."

"Among the humans. My own kind."

"Your own kind are here."

"Why won't you listen to me? You want me to be the perfect Faerie princess, but I'm not! I can't be!"

"Enough."

"Let me go, Father! Let me—"

"Glinfinial, *enough!*" The force of his will hurled her from her feet. "You are my daughter. You will obey me—or face a traitor's fate!"

"Is that supposed to make me beg?" she taunted, scrambling up to face him. "Look you, I know your magic's far stronger than mine, I know you could kill me easily enough. But no matter what you do, you can't make me one bit less human, nor destroy my love for Thierry!"

Raging, he shouted out Words of Binding and saw his daughter stagger, crying out in pain as the magic closed about her. "You are in my Realm," Tiernathal said coolly. "You will stay in this Realm as my daughter or my prisoner, as I choose. Is that understood?"

He watched the helpless rage in Glinfinial's eyes slowly fade to embers as the spell forced obedience on her. "Yes," she murmured.

"Now, leave me!"

As soon as Tiernathal knew himself alone, he sank to a smooth wooden bench, gasping. He would never have let her, or any of his people, know how weary he was, how much the simple act of ensorcelling the humans and dragging back his daughter to him had cost him. But . . . ah, Powers, it had nearly been the end of him!

Tiernathal leaned back against the coolness of a gleaming

marble wall, eyes shut. Once, once he would have been able to crush the humans with the merest flash of will. He could have snatched away whomever he chose with no more effort than a man took to wave an arm. *Once he had stood upon Faerie soil, and felt the magic in Faerie land and air and water rushing through him, so sweet, so splendid—*

Without warning, Forest Heart's words returned to him: Without love, magic has no power. Without warning, he found himself remembering Adele. . . . Adele for whom each new day was a new delight, Adele warm and joyous in his arms—

Oh, ridiculous. Adele had been human. An aberration on his part. He never could have loved her. This mental lapse was merely a result of his weariness.

Weariness that, had things been as they should, he never would be feeling. Tiernathal forced himself to his feet. Moving to the chamber's one window, he leaned on the sill, looking out to where his people danced to the mingling melodies of harp and flute, glancing his way ever so subtly; they must have sensed their ruler's discomfort, and were doing their best to entertain him. But Tiernathal thought their dancing seemed stilted and uncomfortable, and their intricate music harsh to his ears, and after a moment he turned sharply away from the window.

Are they losing even this? he wondered uneasily. *Are my people losing the heart of what it means to be of Faerie?*

Ae, Faerie . . . Remembering the wonder-that-had-been, the wonder that he alone recalled, Tiernathal could almost have cried out in pain. How could his people hold to what they'd been in this foreign Realm, how, when the very land rejected them? If only he could find the lost way home—

But I can't! And I—I don't know what else to do!

Numbly, Tiernathal sank back to the bench. Head in hands, most painfully alone, he surrendered to despair.

SEVEN

The Hunter

"My lord, believe me, my heart goes out to you." Gerard's eyes were so warm with pity that Thierry, pacing wildly to and fro, could hardly bear to glance at them. "But . . . surely you must see this is for the best."

"What? That Glinfinial be snatched away from me? That she—"

"—was of Faerie, my lord. Yes, I agree, she was a sweet lady, a kindhearted lady, but my lord, surely you must admit she just was not truly human! Now she's back with her own people, and you, the count of Foretterre, are free to—"

"To find myself a nice, safe, human wife?" Thierry stopped dead, staring at the steward. "Is that what you're trying to say, Master Gerard? That I should just abandon my lady? Forget I ever met her? You can't possibly believe any of that!"

Gerard let out his breath in a long, weary sigh. "No," he admitted softly. "Of course I don't. But my lord, Thierry, what else *can* you do? We're not talking about merely making a foe of another human nobleman, we're talking about defying a Lord of Faerie! You can't possibly go up against the forces of—of God knows what, and you certainly can't expect any of your men, as much as they may love you, to hazard their souls for you, either."

"They wouldn't. Tiernathal was quite explicit about my going alone. I had no intention of—"

"God in Heaven, Thierry, you *can't* be meaning to try to rescue her all by yourself! That would be the most insane—"

"Then insane I am. Gerard, please. Glinfinial is my heart, my very life." To his embarrassment, Thierry felt his eyes growing moist, and hastily turned away, pretending to be fascinated by the view outside his window. "Without her, I—I—I am nothing, and she—Oh, dear God, who knows what her father may be doing to her?"

"My lord, you cannot help her."

"Didn't you hear a word I said? I can't just abandon her! Tiernathal's of Faerie; he *can't* lie. And he wouldn't have offered me any hope at all if there wasn't a chance that I could win Glinfinial back."

The steward sighed anew. "My lord Thierry, I don't want to overstep my bounds, but if you try to do anything foolish, I swear I will do what I must."

Thierry glared. "Lock me up, you mean? Till my—my madness passes? Then you'd best prepare to be my jailor for a long, long while, because it isn't going to pass! Now—leave me!"

"My lord . . ."

"I said, leave me!"

Gerard left with visible reluctance, but leave he did. Alone, Thierry whirled back to the window, too wild with pent-up energy to know what to do next. Saying he would go after Glinfinial was all well and good, but how was he going to find her in all the forest out there? There might not even be any physical track to follow!

His hand closed convulsively over the little silver crescent-moon pendant, Glinfinial's gift, hanging from its chain around his neck, and felt it warm to his touch, almost as though it smoldered with an inner fire. Odd, odd, the little thing had never felt like this before, almost as though it bore a life of its own, or . . . reflected someone else's life. . . .

Suddenly wondering, Thierry pulled off the chain, placing the pendant carefully down on a table.

And his wild restlessness vanished in that moment.

"Soo . . ." he breathed. Could it be?

He closed his hand about the pendant once more, and all at once was nearly overwhelmed by the urge to be outside, to be searching. Experimenting, Thierry turned this way, that, feeling an inner sense of *rightness* when he faced east—

"Yes, oh, yes! Oh, my clever, clever love!"

The pendant bore magic, no doubt about it! He didn't know if Glinfinial had deliberately bespelled it, or whether the mere fact that it had been worn by one of Faerie blood had been enough, but the pendant was trying, in its own inanimate way, to return to her.

"And so you'll lead me right to her, won't you?" Thierry said, and laughed aloud.

The most difficult part had been stealing out of the manor house and away from his estate, trying to move smoothly and silently in his forester's plain leather tunic and trousers and thick woolen cloak as a shadow in the night, bow and pack doing their best to trip him up. Thank Heaven that night had been moonless! Not daring to strike a light even when he'd struggled from cultivated land into the forest, he'd snagged clothes and skin on branches and nearly broken his neck tripping over exposed roots before he'd found a cozy spot at the base of an ancient beech and actually managed to get some sleep.

Now, in the cool gray light of early morning, with thick forest all around him, alive with birdsong and the rustling of leaves, Thierry felt more rested than he'd expected, lying blinking sleepily up at the swaying branches overhead.

Ah, enough of this. He must be off. Gerard was surely going to send out men looking for him, but once he reached deep forest, Thierry was confident enough in his woodcraft to know he could avoid them. All he had to worry about was losing the pendant. Or himself. Or his life and soul.

"Oh, is *that* all?" Thierry murmured wryly.

He rose from his makeshift bed of leaves, shivering in the still-chilly air, jumping about to warm himself up and try to stretch the stiffness out of his muscles. Half afraid he might have lost it in the night's struggle, Thierry reached up a hasty hand to touch Glinfinial's pendant, and smiled to feel its warmth steal through his hand, telling him as clearly as any words, *This way, she passed this way.*

The count took a deep breath of clean, spicy-sweet forest air. "Forward," he said.

Thierry sank to a fallen tree, head in hands. How many days had he been traveling? How many days of struggling through forest so dense he wasn't sure he'd be able to find his way out? He'd been so full of hope when he'd started out, but now . . .

Ah, Glinfinial, what am I going to do? How am I ever going to find you?

The ironic thing about all this despair was that physically he was perfectly comfortable. The weather had stayed obligingly warm and dry, his muscles had toughened up quickly, and he'd been sleeping well enough each night on the bough-and-leaf beds a forester had long ago taught him how to make. There were edible plants and berries for the taking, a wealth of rabbits for anyone quick with a bow, and fish to be scooped from the streams; Thierry knew the trick of letting his hand loll in the water, lulling the fish till there was a chance to pounce.

I probably would be enjoying myself, if only, if only—

"Curse you, Tiernathal!" he yelled in sudden defiance. "I will not let you win!"

All around him, the forest fell into shocked silence, and just for a moment Thierry dared believe his melodramatic shout might somehow have broken a Faerie spell.

But after that startled moment, the normal little chirpings and stirrings resumed, and the young man sighed and lowered his head to his hands once more. He had been tracking back and forth through this same patch of forest for what seemed a lifetime, *knowing* Glinfinial was nearby, just out of reach, *knowing* the way to her had to be here, somewhere in this narrow strip of land, and yet seeing not the slightest clue. No matter how he approached it, how many times he crossed through it, there was nothing that distinguished this land from the rest of the forest, nothing to see but trees and trees and trees even though the pendant was silently screaming, *Here! She's here!* and practically burning his skin with its frantic warmth.

"Curse you, Tiernathal," Thierry repeated helplessly, more softly this time, and got to his feet. Around him, the forest was rapidly darkening with the onset of yet another night, and the count wearily set about making camp once more. A chill gust of wind made him shiver and glance up.

Wonderful. The fine weather was changing rapidly, and what glimpses of sky he could catch through the canopy of leaves was growing heavily cloud laden.

Is that your doing, too, Faerie Lord? Thierry thought wryly. *Can you control the weather, too?*

As though mocking him, a sudden blinding flash of lightning and roar of thunder made him start and look hastily around for shelter. Under a tree was hardly the best place to be during a thunderstorm, but there didn't seem to be much choice about it, particularly since the racing storm clouds were making it almost too dark to see where he was going.

"Oh, *damn!*"

The rain had come pouring down, soaking him before he could pull his cloak about him and its hood over his head. A second flash blazed across the sky, for an instant turning the forest to an eerie, blue-white world, leaving him dazzled, filling his nose with the sharp tang of lightning-torn air, and the trees shook with the force of the thunder. Thierry did the only thing he could do, and crouched low to the ground to present as small a target as possible while the storm tore itself apart around him.

There. After an eternity of noise and wet, it seemed to be

moving on at last. At least the sky was brightening and the rain had nearly stopped—

His world exploded with a roar and blare of light, and Thierry went flying, ending up with a thud against a reassuringly solid trunk. Shaking, he struggled to catch his breath. God, that had been close! One last blast of lightning had struck a tree so close to him that it was a miracle he hadn't been charred! He could see the smoke of the strike, and smell the acrid tang of burning—

—and oh, the terror, the blind, mindless, terror blazing through him!

Thierry drew back with a gasp, trying to fight off the choking waves of panic sweeping over him. This was ridiculous, he was safe, there was nothing to fear, these—

—weren't his thoughts, weren't his fear, the fear, ah, the fear, no one to help, no one!

Bewildered, frightened, knowing he couldn't *not* investigate, Thierry prowled cautiously forward. He could see the lightning-riven tree by its own light; it had been split nearly in two, and the fallen half was burning brightly.

And someone was caught under it! Thierry raced forward, tearing off his cloak, beating at the flames, smothering them with desperate handfuls of earth. For all the drama, the fire hadn't gotten too much of a head start, and at last, panting, he gasped out, "Th-there. It's out. Are—are you hurt?"

But the figure, whoever, whatever it was, had already managed to struggle free, disappearing into shadow before Thierry had gotten more than one bewildering flash of what might have been fur, or feathers, or even scales.

"What in the name of . . ."

"You saved the forest." It was a strange whisper, more like the sound of branches scraping together in the wind, smooth and harsh in one. "You saved me."

"You're quite welcome," Thierry said uncertainly. "But . . . who . . . are you?"

The dry, rustling sound might have been a chuckle.

"Who? What? Forest Heart am I, the forest am I. It is not often that the forest, that I, need be indebted to a human."

Too confused for speech, Thierry fell back on courtesy, and bowed. He heard the rustling chuckle rasp out of the darkness, then the being, the forest's soul, the whatever, added, "What would you?"

"I wasn't thinking of reward! I couldn't leave anyone to die like that!"

"Ahh, no . . . Forest Heart, the forest, I fear the Fire, the enemy Element. . . ." The eerie voice sank to the barest whisper. "Had I, had Forest Heart, been slain by flame, the forest would have died as well. . . . So! This was a great deed you did, forest-friend, fire slayer. Come, what would you?"

Overwhelmed, Thierry said the first thing that came to mind: "Please, help me reach my lady!"

But would a creature of elemental Power want to side with a magicless human against Faerie? Not daring to think what might happen if Forest Heart, who seemed somehow to be the very soul of the forest, turned against him, the young man stammered out the rest of his story.

"The Faerie Lord . . ." It was a speculative whisper. "So, and so . . ."

All around them, the forest seemed to be holding its breath, waiting. Thierry felt the quiet strength of it, and for the first time feared that strength. But then Forest Heart chuckled.

"Yes. Come."

A . . . hand? Was it a hand that closed about his wrist? It seemed to prickle with thorns and be smooth and hard as stone, but before he could steal a good look at it, Thierry was being dragged back through the patch of forest he'd so futilely crossed again and again.

"Wait, this can't—it won't . . ."

But it wasn't the forest. Or rather, it wasn't quite the *same* forest. The trees were more widely spaced, and beyond them he thought he saw a hint of a gently sloping meadow.

It was difficult to judge distance or detail in the soft blue twilight light that filled the air.

"This is the Faerie Lord's Realm," whispered Forest Heart. "Walk warily."

Thierry whirled—but the being was gone. He was alone in the twilight, standing beneath a tranquil, sunless sky.

EIGHT

In a Strange Land

Glinfinial sat in her father's small rose garden, surrounded by neatly rounded bushes, each bespelled to be exactly like the next, each bearing a rich display of ever-blooming pure white blossoms, and tried her best to ignore her two half sisters strolling languidly down a garden path. They were almost alike enough to be twins, tall, slim, and elegant in true Faerie fashion, one in palest green, one in softest blue, their hair falling in sleek silvery waves down their backs. They were whispering together, carefully, just loudly enough for her to overhear them.

"She wanted to live with *them!*" Scorn dripped from Tareniel's voice. She waved a graceful arm in contempt, her long green sleeve floating in the still air. "She actually wanted to *marry* one of them! Think of the disgrace that would have brought upon all of us!"

"Oh, but my dear, what can you expect?" Serenial murmured. "That's her human side showing. What more *can* you expect of a poor little half blood?"

That I show my human side, Glinfinial thought, hands clenched, *by slapping both of you, you spiteful little cats.*

No. She wasn't going to give them the satisfaction of seeing that they'd hurt her. She certainly wasn't going to let them see her weep from sheer frustration, missing Thierry, worrying about him, yet being able to do nothing about it thanks to her father's spell! Oh, Glinfinial was free to roam within the intricate, everchanging halls of his estate. But if she so much as tried to put a foot across the barriers Tiernathal had set, she ran into invisible but very real walls.

He can't keep me here forever!

Couldn't he? His Power was so much stronger than hers.

Glinfinial grinned a sudden fierce little grin. Her father was forgetting one thing: Weaker didn't necessarily mean helpless. What if she kept her magics small, innocent, beneath his notice? . . . Yes, oh, yes!

Tareniel and Serenial, seeing that she wasn't going to respond to their taunts, were strolling off in an artfully graceful swirl of silken gowns. Glinfinial watched, doing nothing else, till they were out of sight, then waited with true Faerie patience, sitting more still than the bushes around her, keeping her mind a careful blank, till she was sure that no one was watching. Only then did she move, ever so slowly and casually, to a small, quiet pool, sitting on its rim as though lost in thought.

Slipping open the silver brooch clasping her cloak, hiding what she did in the silvery folds of material, Glinfinial jabbed her finger, refusing to wince, then let fall one, two, three drops of blood into the water. Her hand trailed in the pool, so languidly that no one would have noticed she was stirring the water in one, two, three spirals with her hand, whispering as she did quiet, subtle Words, whispering after that, "Thierry, Thierry, Thierry . . ."

It was the simplest, most primitive of scrying charms, so primitive that her father and sisters would never deign to use it, or even remember it existed, so slight a charm that it slid beneath the walls of her father's Spell of Binding without stirring them.

"Thierry, Thierry, Thierry . . . Let me see him, let me see, let me . . ."

There! He looked ragged and unkempt in the twilight, as though he'd been trekking through forest for uncounted days. And oh, was that a tender new beard on his chin? Glinfinial bit back a giggle, trying irrelevantly to decide if she liked it or not. At least he looked healthy, and unharmed. And it was wonderfully comforting to realize he was hunting *her*, even if he could never find the way. . . .

Couldn't he? Surely the dim blue light surrounding him was never that of mortal twilight.

"Oh, Thierry, no!"

How could he have entered her father's lands? And oh, Powers help him, how was he ever going to survive the dangers here?

He couldn't, not alone. Spell of Binding or no, she must get out there and help him! Glinfinial straightened, thinking nervously of Tiernathal's anger, wondering, *Can I do it? Do I dare?*

She didn't *not* dare, not if she ever meant to see her love alive.

Thierry looked about in confusion, trying to clear his mind. There really wasn't a sun in the sky. Or at least, he couldn't see the faintest hint of sunlight penetrating the thick blue haze. Yet, sun or no sun, this was still the forest. The trees all around him were the same types he'd grown up knowing, and the way they thinned out ahead into meadowland wasn't out of the natural way of things, either: Fire, long ago, might have led to just that sort of slow regrowth from bare earth to grass. Eventually saplings would spring up, and the meadow would return to forest—

Stop babbling! he snapped at himself. *This is hardly the time for a nature lesson!*

All at once Thierry knew what was making him uneasy besides the unlikely twilight. The snatches of birdsong he heard were just too musical, too perfect, almost as though the birds had been tuned like so many feathery musical instruments. The soft, still air was just a touch too fragrant to be true. And how could the trees be retaining their leaves?

How, when they couldn't be getting much in the way of sunlight thanks to this eerie blue twilight?

The answer brought a shiver rippling up his spine: Magic. No way around it. This was the forest, yes, or part of the forest, but with Tiernathal's spells laid upon it.

Tiernathal's Realm. Thierry closed his hand about Glinfinial's silver pendant, and felt it reassuringly warm. Forest Heart—whoever, whatever—had pointed him in the right direction. Glinfinial was somewhere ahead of him.

"And I'll find you, love," he murmured.

But his balance felt odd.

My quiver—my bow—My whole pack is gone!

More alarming, his sword was gone, too, and his belt knife. Every bit of Faerie-hating iron had been taken from him.

Wonderful, just wonderful. Not only was he a stranger in a very foreign Realm, he was unarmed as well.

Ah, well, he hadn't *really* expected things to be too easy! Thierry took a deep, resigned breath of the too-soft, too-sweet air, and started forward once more.

Something was stalking him. Thierry, making his way down what he assumed was a deer path, glanced from side to side as casually as he could, but saw nothing. And yet it was there, he knew it, he *felt* it as surely as any hunted wild thing, even though whatever his pursuer was, animal, human, or Faerie, it was skillful enough to make not the slighest sound.

Thierry bent as though to adjust a boot. His hand closed on a stout fallen branch, and he straightened, hefting it experimentally. A good weight, and it seemed strong wood. The faintest rustle of leaves made him whirl, heart racing, to see—

No! Impossible!

A spider out of a nightmare lunged up before him, dead black and nearly as huge as a man. Long, curving mandibles clashing, it leapt at him, compound eyes like glittering beads of jet, and Thierry swung the branch with all his might.

The spider vanished. The force of his swing spun Thierry around, sending him stumbling down into the middle of a prickly bush. Gasping, he struggled to free himself from the web of leaves and branches, trying to get his legs under him, twisting to stare back to where the spider lurked, waiting. Surely that couldn't be a hint of shrill laughter he heard? Spiders didn't laugh, or grow to the size of men, either!

Thierry let out his breath in a sharp hiss. Of course they didn't! He had grown up hearing Simon's tales of magical beings, after all. And now that he had a moment to gather his wits, Thierry remembered the old man telling him about the *lutin*, a small trickster who delighted in fooling humans with false shapes.

"All right, Master Lutin," Thierry called, trying to keep his voice light and cheerful, "you've had your fun. I must have looked deliciously silly landing in this bush. But we both know spiders don't grow so large—and don't dissolve into mist when a man tries to hit them!"

For a heartstopping moment the spider still loomed over him, and he had just time enough to wonder if he'd made a fatal mistake. Then it melted into empty air. A new peal of shrill, delighted laughter rang out, then the *lutin*, a small, vaguely man-shaped figure clad in bits of bark, scurried away into the forest. Thierry finally managed to scramble to his feet, shaking off bits of branch and leaf, staring after the vanished being in wonder.

At least the pranksters hadn't really meant him any real harm. *Lutins* seldom did, or so Simon had assured him, not if their human victims were polite enough to laugh along with them. If shape-shifting jokers were the worst this land had to throw at him, there wasn't much to fear, twilight strangeness or no!

Shouldering his makeshift staff, Thierry strode forward.

The movement saved him. Something large, heavy, and undeniably not illusory went hurtling past him, just missing him, disappearing into the bushes with a crash. Staff clutched in both hands, Thierry whirled to where it had disappeared, poised on the balls of his feet, heart racing anew, waiting for a new attack.

But nothing happened. All that came out of the bushes was . . . a whining? A plaintive whining, such as a frightened hound might make? Thierry warily parted the bushes with his makeshift staff, hands shaking, expecting whatever was lurking in there to leap out at him. . . .

"Saints in Heaven—it *is* a hound!"

Not much of one: a dirty white hunting hound so skinny he could nearly count its ribs. As he stared down at it, his heartbeat gradually returning to normal, the hound looked up at him with limpid brown eyes, the tip of its tail moving in a tentative wag.

"Well," Thierry managed at last. "It certainly wasn't *you* who attacked me!"

At the sound of his voice, the hound flattened itself in canine submission, whimpering and wriggling, tail continuing its hesitant wagging. Thierry straightened, glancing warily about, looking and listening with all his might.

Nothing. That predatory Other was gone.

"Whatever attacked was much bigger than you, hound. Not big enough to take me for prey, saints be praised. Must have bowled you right over in its haste to get away, eh, boy?"

The hound panted, tongue lolling in a canine smile. Thierry crouched by the dog's side, warily offering it a hand to sniff, grinning as that tongue swiped at his arm. "You're a human's hound, aren't you? You must be! Sorry, dog, but I doubt any Faerie Lord would want such a scrawny beast in his kennels! No, you must have somehow fallen through the . . . uh . . . barrier, same as me. And now you're as lost in this wherever-we-are as I am." He patted the thin head. "Sorry, I can't return you to your owner."

He stood, and the hound scrambled up, tail wagging so frantically that the thin body shook. "Want to come with me, boy? Is that what you're trying to say? All right, then, come on. I'll be glad of the company."

Company the dog was, following at his heels like a well-trained lady's pet, never taking its gaze from him. It didn't seem to be much of a hunting hound, though, staring at him blankly, never even twitching an ear when he tried to get it to chase a rabbit. Thierry sighed as the rabbit vanished, untouched, into the underbrush, and shook his head at the hound.

"Aren't you getting hungry, dog? *I* am. These berries may be tasty"—and fortunately seemed to be as normal as the trees—"but they're not exactly filling." The dog continued to stare at him, tongue lolling. "What's the matter, boy?" Thierry asked. "Don't you *like* to hunt?" He sighed again, peering around in the increasingly dim light. "Not that it matters now. It's going to be night pretty soon, so let's see what we can do about making camp."

It didn't take long. Without food, without bedding, without flint and steel—ah, well, he'd camped out in worse conditions. At least the air was warm, soft, and dry, and he could still make a halfway decent bough bed for himself. It wouldn't hurt him to go to bed a bit hungry, either. With all this greenery, there must surely be streams, and tomorrow he would see about snatching himself some fish. . . .

Tomorrow . . .

Thierry was nearly asleep when a shrill peal of laughter woke him with a start.

Eyes! Blazing green eyes and glinting fangs—the hound! *Oh, you idiot*, Thierry's mind screamed, *how could you ever take it for a little lost dog?* Hound no longer, it had grown huge and hungry, ghostly white in the darkness, snarling its anger because he'd awakened before it could attack.

"You—*galipote!*" Thierry identified it, and lunged upward with his staff from where he lay. The galipote, the hound-like, shape-shifting predator, sprang back in alarm; just as stories told, it plainly preferred smaller, defenseless prey. Thierry sprang up, swinging the staff like a broadsword, and the *galipote* cringed back again, snarling, then straightened. It gave him a brief, almost wistful look, as though it were thinking, What a wonderfully *big* meal you would have made!

Then it turned and fled. Thierry stood panting for a moment, grinning at that last message despite himself. But then his smile faded and he sank back to the ground. Saints, saints, first a *lutin*, then a *galipote.* Were all the tales Simon had ever told him going to come true? And that hound had seemed so real, so—so *safe!* Could he trust nothing?

He could trust Glinfinial. Thierry closed his hand on the little pendant, and smiled at its reassuring warmth. Still smiling, he settled back on his makeshift bed.

But he slept very little that night.

NINE

The Chase

Tiernathal sat alone in his private chambers, in a room of blank, pearl gray walls, sat before a smooth pane of silvered glass, staring without emotion at his reflection, acknowledging with true Faerie fatalism that though his face was as unmarked by time as always, ever-increasing hints of strain burned in his eyes.

After a moment, impatient, the Faerie Lord gestured, and his reflection blurred, then disappeared as the mirror's surface grayed. For a moment fog seemed to swirl up behind the flat surface, then the mirror cleared once more, revealing a twilight-hued forest scene in miniature, and the human moving within it.

Tiernathal hissed, ever so softly. Of course he had known Thierry was in his lands; the Faerie Lord had been aware of that unwelcome presence from the moment the human had first crossed his magical boundaries. But he'd seen no immediate need to act. Why waste precious magic to destroy such a petty creature, even one so ridiculously persistent? Humans had no sense of subtlety or caution. Surely this one would manage to destroy himself.

Yet so far Thierry had proven himself surprisingly wise in the old ways, recognizing *lutin* and *galipote* for what they were, knowing to be polite to the one and just threatening enough to the other. And he'd already come a surprising distance.

Wait, now . . . Tiernathal mused for a bit, narrow chin resting on steepled fingers. What if that incredible human stubbornness could be somehow put to use? Surely there was something—Powers, yes! The Faerie Lord straightened as sharply as though he'd been slapped, all at once thinking of three most intriguing artifacts, Powerful things that just might hold vital clues within them. The magic within them was so shaped that no one truly of Faerie could capture them, and so, up till now, he had fought down his frustration to the point where he'd put them from his mind.

Until now. Thierry was most definitely not of Faerie. And with the force of Glinfinial's love to strengthen him—

Glinfinial, whom Thierry was trying to steal. Tiernathal's lips tightened with distaste. No matter what the cost, he was *not* about to make things simple for that thieving human! There were other beings in his Realm than mere *galipotes*, beings not so lightly chased away. The Faerie Lord gestured anew, murmuring sharp-edged words of command, and settled back in his high-backed chair, fingers comfortably steepled once more, and continued to watch.

Morning—or what passed for morning in that sunless place—found a bleary-eyed, yawning Thierry using his staff as a walking stick, making his way out of forest across a wide, apparently natural meadow. He must have slept for at least a short time, because he'd awakened to find his hair knotted into plaits: a *lutin* prank. One or more of the small beings seemed, in their mischievous way, to have befriended him.

At least *someone* here felt friendly toward him. Thierry was growing heartily sick of this endless twilight, of this warm, soft, nearly breathless air, of this never quite satisfying diet of berries—of everything to do with this Realm!

All at once, as though it had materialized out of air, a huge black figure appeared at the meadow's far edge, so eerily familiar in outline that Thierry's first thought was a bewildered, *Goliath?* From this distance, it did look very much like an enormous bull pawing the ground, its horns like two great curving swords.

But as the monster suddenly charged, moving swiftly as a racing horse for all its bulk, Thierry saw that scales glinted along its sides, and taloned feet bit deeply into the ground, sending clods of earth flying. Flame red eyes blazed from a fanged face that was more horrifying for being almost human, and all at once Thierry realized this could only be the creature out of nightmare known as the Tarasque, demonic eater of flesh. Oh, Lord, and every one of Simon's tales of the creature had an unhappy ending for its mortal prey. There wasn't any way a mere human could defeat it, those tales all claimed. And for a moment Thierry could only stand, staring, racking his brain for any solution at all, as death came thundering toward him.

I'll never be able to outrun him! But how can I possibly fight with nothing more than a branch?

There wasn't much else he could do. As the Tarasque lowered its terrible head, horns dagger sharp, Thierry braced himself, remembering how he'd battled Goliath, trying to ignore the inner voice clamoring that this wasn't any mortal bull, this was a demon thing.

At the last possible moment, the hot stench of the beast choking him, he threw himself to one side. As he'd hoped, the Tarasque thundered helplessly past. But it stopped and whirled far more swiftly than any mortal beast, charging Thierry once more before he could even get to his feet. Thierry lunged from a crouch, staff held out like a lance, his only hope to catch the Tarasque in a blazing eye, but the wood splintered against the monster's scales. He heard the breath leave his lungs as a hard shoulder crashed into him, sending him tumbling to the ground. Aching, Thierry struggled to rise, even though he knew it wasn't going to make much difference whether he stood or not. Either way, he was going to be gored or trampled, either way he was going to die.

But cursed if he was going to die meekly!

As the Tarasque thundered down on him, Thierry caught one huge horn, letting it pull him even as he leaped up with all his might—and landed astride the beast. For one wild, breathless moment, he felt all that incredible, alien power beneath him. Then the outraged Tarasque roared and with one mighty lunge sent Thierry flying. Earth and sky spun together crazily, then he hit the ground so hard that he could do nothing but lie where he'd fallen and gasp for air. Behind him, he heard the Tarasque gathering itself for one final charge.

"Tarasque!" shouted a fierce voice, and Thierry managed to raise himself on an elbow, turning to see.

Glinfinial! She stood with royal pride, hair flying wildly about her pale blue gown, so lovely, so alien, so truly of Faerie that the breath caught in Thierry's throat. For all her will, she looked so small against the bulk of the Tarasque, and yet, though the monster snorted smoke and pawed the ground impatiently, it dared not approach. Glinfinial shouted a command in the liquid, twisting Faerie tongue, once and yet again, green eyes blazing.

It will never obey, Thierry thought. *It's going to attack, and I—* But then, with a reluctant glare at Thierry, the Tarasque turned and cantered heavily away.

After a moment's tension, the cold inhumanity faded from Glinfinial. She sagged in relief and threw herself down at Thierry's side. And for a time they could do nothing but hug each other as though they'd never let go.

But at last Glinfinial drew back, staring at Thierry. "My love, are you all right? Are you hurt? Let me—"

"I'm all right, truly, just bruised a bit. But how did you—where did you—Glinfinial, where did you come from? I mean, how did you appear so suddenly?"

"There's a tiny trick of magic, illusion to make one seem clear as air, using fern seed—"

"But ferns don't *have* seeds!"

She gave him the faintest hint of a grin. "That's the trick of it! But it's such a small, such a silly little spell, it was too small for my father to even notice." Glinfinial stiffened, staring. "Or it was. Thierry, I think he just realized I'm missing!" She scrambled to her feet in sudden panic, pulling him up with her. "He mustn't find us! Hurry, love, we must run!"

Her terror was contagious. Hand in hand, they raced back through the forest, Glinfinial moving as smoothly as a wood sprite, Thierry stumbling over roots in his haste, feeling thorns snag clothes and skin, biting back an oath as a branch slapped him neatly across the face, bringing tears to his eyes.

"Glinfinial, we can't—I can't—"

"We must!" she gasped. "Please! The Gate isn't too far ahead!"

I hope you mean the Gate back to the normal, sunlit, unmagical *world!* he thought, too breathless for speech.

Gritting his teeth, Thierry hurried after her. How big *was* this Realm? Even with the weight of Tiernathal's magic on it, it was still only forest, part of the forest he knew, and yet it seemed endless. Surely they were going to keep running beneath that accursed twilight haze forever.

Glinfinial's startled scream brought Thierry up short, panting, fumbling at his side for the sword that wasn't there. Out of the shadows before them were materializing a dozen Faerie warriors, their lean, fair faces grim. Silvery mail shone supple as fish scales, silvery blades glinted in steady hands.

"I think we have a problem," Thierry murmured in wry understatement. Wondering if they even understood the human tongue, he added warily to the warriors, "Look you, we mean you no harm, we mean no harm to this land. Can you understand me? We only want to go home and . . . oh. Never mind."

The line of warriors parted. A tall, slender, fiercely beautiful man, ageless and splendid in silver robes, stepped soundlessly forward: Tiernathal. Thierry recognized him from that magic-induced dream. Green eyes opaque and cold as winter ice, the Faerie Lord glanced at his wild-eyed daughter, snapping out something in his native tongue.

"No," Glinfinial said defiantly. "Speak so that Thierry can understand."

Tiernathal's glance said that the human wasn't even worth contempt. "So be it. Daughter, return."

"To what? A life that can never really be mine? Father, you must accept this: I've more of human than Faerie in me. And I've chosen to follow my mother's blood."

Tiernathal's face was very still. "No."

"It's not something you can decide for me. Father, I—I'm sorry, I don't want to hurt you, but please, you know there's no place for me here!"

She glanced at Thierry, eyes so full of anguish that he ached to take her in his arms. But he could hardly do that in front of Tiernathal, so Thierry contented himself with closing his hand on hers, trying to will reassurance into her. And he saw some of the anguish fade. Glinfinial gave him a fleeting smile, then turned back to her father.

"No," she said quietly. "I cannot return. My place is with Thierry."

Tiernathal merely gestured, murmuring Words that hurt Thierry's ears. Glinfinial cried out briefly in protest—

And then she was gone, as easily as that, empty air rushing in to fill the space she had just occupied, staggering Thierry.

"No," he gasped, and then, "Curse you, no! What have you—"

He stopped short as those silvery sword points pricked him; Faerie warriors had moved swiftly and silently up behind him.

"Did you think I would harm her?" Tiernathal asked, voice coolly controlled. "I am not a human, to hurt my own blood. And she *is* my daughter, deny it though she will. This time she shall not find it so easy to elude me, that is all. But you . . ."

If those green, never-human eyes had only burned with hatred, Thierry could have borne it. But all he could read was a cold indifference that seemed somehow much more terrible than any hate. Oh, God, let this alien, alien creature not see how scared he was. . . . The only comfort he could take was in the faint sag of weariness to Tiernathal's shoulders; magicking away his daughter couldn't have been easy.

I hope it drained all the Power from you, you arrogant . . .

Not that the Faerie Lord was going to need magic to be rid of him. One lunge with a warrior's sword would take care of that.

Thierry swallowed drily. "If you're going to kill me," he said as defiantly as he could, "go ahead, get it over with."

One elegant eyebrow lifted ever so slightly. "Did I say anything about killing you? No. Or at least not yet. I challenge you, human. Is that not what your kind would say? I challenge you."

"But I don't have any—"

"No, fool, not with weapons! I could slay you with a thought before you could raise a blade!"

"What, then?"

"I offer you three Tests, human." The way the word was emphasized left no doubt in Thierry's mind that it was meant to be capitalized. "Pass them," Tiernathal continued, "and you and Glinfinial shall be safe, my word upon it. Fail them . . ." The Faerie Lord shrugged, a small, inhumanly graceful movement. "Fail them, and *then* you shall die. Is that clear enough, human?"

"Quite clear," Thierry snapped. "You had this whole thing planned from the start, didn't you?"

"No. From the start I merely watched, curious. But when I saw my daughter defy me, hurry to rescue you—" Tiernathal stopped short, and Thierry felt a little twinge of satisfaction at having forced this so-cool being to show something as common as rage. "Then," the Faerie Lord continued in a voice once more coolly controlled, "I realized what could be done. And so, the Tests.

"First: Bring me the Acorn of Knowledge from the Oak of Gwailahier."

"The—the what?"

"Second," Tiernathal continued unheeding, "Bring me the Jewel of Thought from the *guibre*."

"I don't even know what a *guibre is*!"

"And third: Bring me the Pearl of Farsight from the Lady of the Moor."

"B-but this is ridiculous! It's like a quest in some stupid minstrel's song! And I—"

"Are you refusing?"

There was the faintest thread of warning in the simple words, just enough to send a shiver through Thierry. "I didn't say that," he hedged. "But where—"

"Can they be found? That," said Tiernathal coolly, "is for you to learn."

Without another word, he turned and, together with his warriors, faded into the forest.

TEN

Fatherly Love

"How could you do this to us? How *dare* you do this?"

Tiernathal frowned in distaste at his daughter's outburst. Granted, she must still be shaken, disheveled and panting as she was from having been snatched from forest back to the Faerie Lord's mansion, but that was no excuse for such mannerless fury.

"Stop that!" he said sternly. "Remember to whom you speak. I am your father!"

"Father!" she snapped. "You act more like a—a master! Treating me like a slave, no, like a mindless beast, a *thing*, snatching me away from Thierry—"

"The fool of a human."

"The man I love! The man who loves me!"

"What nonsense."

He watched Glinfinial struggle to choke down her rage. "Father," she said in a voice that shook, "I am not a child. You had no right to drag me off against my will."

"It was for your own sake."

"Oh, really? Is kidnaping the way a father shows his love?"

Tiernathal stirred impatiently. "What has love to do with it? You are the daughter of a Faerie Lord, no matter how . . . debased your blood, and you cannot be permitted to foul yourself with that human."

"As you fouled yourself with my mother?"

"Be silent!" he hissed, so savagely that he saw her flinch. But she continued defiantly, "And here I always thought you loved her, somewhere deep inside you. But you really don't care, do you? You never cared." Trembling, she wrapped her arms tightly about herself. "Even at the worst of times, even when I knew you despised my human blood, I—I never doubted that you loved me. But now . . ." Glinfinial's eyes were very bright. "Why, what a fool I've been not to have realized. I really am no more to you than a possession."

"That's ridiculous."

"Is it? Come, I challenge you: If you do love me, if you care what becomes of me—let me go. Accept me for what I am and let me live my own life."

"As a human? Glinfinial, you could not bear it. You would grow old, you would die. . . ."

"I know. I've thought about it many a night. But if that's part of what it means to be human, so be it."

Tiernathal turned sharply away. "You talk so lightly of something you don't understand."

"At least in the human world I would have a chance to *live* before I died! Here, I'm just a curiosity, the Faerie Lord's sadly tainted daughter, someone to be whispered about behind her back."

"None would dare."

"Oh, wouldn't they? You haven't even noticed, have you? You're so busy pretending this sad little imitation Realm is Faerie that you don't—"

"Enough!" It was a shout of pain.

Glinfinial winced. "I'm sorry. I didn't mean to say that."

"The matter is ended! You will *not* go off to live like a beast."

"Father—"

"This foolishness will pass. After all, you are not the first of Faerie to have been infatuated with a human."

"Were *you* nothing but infatuated? Am I only the result of infatuation?"

He refused to reply. "I've wasted enough time with you.

You *will* stay here, you *will* honor your Faerie blood—and you will not argue with me again!"

Without warning, he attacked, meaning to cast the net of a Binding Spell about her before she could react. But to his astonishment, her small Power rose in a wild wave to meet his, staggering him, surging against his will. Off-balance, almost overwhelmed by that desperate ferocity, Tiernathal found himself forced to defend himself, calling up deeper Power, hurling her own magics back on her. Her strength was crumbling beneath his. . . .

With one last surge of will, Glinfinial screamed, physically and mentally, "Thierry! Thierry! North, turn north!"

And then she fell.

Frozen in horror for what seemed an eternity, Tiernathal could do nothing but stare down at his daughter's still form. Powers, Powers, had he hurt her? Had he . . . killed her?

No. At last he realized that she still breathed. And that breathing was normal, the patterns of her mind unaltered. He stood swaying over her for a time, struggling to catch his breath, then steeled himself and bent, picking up her slight form. Weary though he was, the Binding Spell must be finished now, before she recovered, or there'd be all this to do over again.

". . . *aetherin'ah, las'terial!*"

It was done. Tiernathal rubbed a hand over his eyes, feeling himself trembling with strain, then turned to look back at his daughter, his Glinfinial, where she lay wrapped in magical slumber till he should choose to break his spell. And for a moment, all that he could think was that her bed looked most wonderfully soft. . . .

Nonsense. Tiernathal rubbed his eyes again, willing away the ache to sleep as best he could. Surely fresh air would help as well as any restorative magics. He moved with exaggerated care to a window and leaned on the sill, drinking in the soft air, eyes shut.

The sound of twittering voices broke the quiet. He

glanced down to see Tareniel and Serenial, his two children of the true blood, strolling together, arm in arm. Bits of their light, idle, delicately malicious gossip drifted up to him, and he straightened in sudden distaste. Trivial creatures! Why must it be that his only daughter with strength, with fire, with pride, the only daughter worthy of him, should be the one whose blood was tainted?

The one who longed to leave him.

And for what? The sordid human life? The life in which she would wither like a flower? Where, as he'd warned her, she would even die? . . .

Ae, Powers!

Tiernathal forced his mind away from the unexpected stab of memory, from Adele. Adele, who had died so young, leaving him alone. . . .

No! He could not grieve for a human, he would not!

Slowly Tiernathal urged his pounding heart to calmness, cooled his raging mind to stillness. Icily composed at last, he stalked from the chamber, intent on his magic mirror, intent on watching Thierry.

Did he wish the human success or failure? Tiernathal shook his head, bemused. He'd designed those Tests with care, and either way, the results would be . . . intriguing. Were Thierry to fail, as seemed most likely, he would die, and the threat of Glinfinial's loss would be ended. But were Thierry by some miracle to succeed, were he really to return with the Acorn of Knowledge, the Jewel of Thought, the Pearl of Farsight . . .

The Faerie Lord shivered, all at once nearly overwhelmed by a sudden painful surge of longing. Ah, what bitter irony! For all his need, he had been blocked from stealing those artifacts himself; no one of true Faerie blood could do so. That he should be dependent on a human!

But if Thierry were to win the precious things for him, what matter the shame? For who knew but that the artifacts might hold the most lost, most precious secret of all: the one true path back to Faerie?

ELEVEN

Oak and Acorn

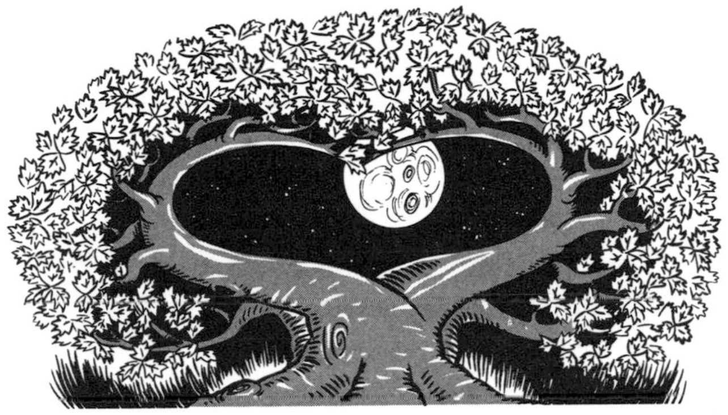

Thierry stood in confused despair, alone in twilight-dim forest. Had he really heard Glinfinial's voice touch his mind, screaming, *North, turn north*? North? How in the name of all the saints did one tell north from any other direction when he couldn't see the sun?

"Oh, idiot, by the stars, of course!"

Last night, the canopy of trees had effectively cut off the sky. And he hadn't been in any condition to go stargazing! But the twilight dimness wasn't exactly a cloud; perhaps it faded with the coming of darkness. The stories never said that the Faerie folk had a quarrel with starlight, after all.

He could hope.

He must.

Hours later, that hope was repaid. Heart racing, Thierry stared up at the night sky, picking out blessedly familiar constellations, and gave a shout of laughter at the sight of the North Star so clearly pointing out the way he must go.

North Thierry went, and north again, using the forester's trick of sighting in a straight line from tree to tree to keep himself going in the right direction once the twilight-hued day had returned. There wasn't the slightest sign of a threat from animal or Other. In fact, there wasn't a sign of animal life at all, save for the occasional distant twitter of a bird. Fortunate, then, that the berries, no matter how unsatisfying a diet they might be, seemed to have enough Faerie magic in them to be as nourishing as any true dinner. The occasional familiar herb or root gave him a chance to satisfy the need to chew something solid.

And I'm not going to believe those stupid tales that claim anyone who eats food in the Otherworld never returns to human Realms.

But oh, for a joint of roast venison. Or a loaf of bread hot from the oven, spread with butter . . .

A spider strand slipped smoothly across his mouth, so smoothly he could have sworn a hand put it there, and Thierry sputtered and brushed it away. A hand, indeed! He'd suspected a *lutin* or, for all he knew, a whole tribe of *lutins*, had been trailing him all day, because every time he let his mind wander, leaves would somehow slip down his neck, or knots mysteriously plait themselves into his hair, or acorns drop with perfect aim onto his head.

Thierry grinned. These might be small nuisances, but at the same time there was something strangely comforting about them, like the jokes played by a well-meaning prankster friend.

"Now, if only you would stop playing those jokes long enough to point out the Oak of Gwailahier," he told his unseen followers, only half joking himself.

"There," said a high, shrill voice, and "There," echoed a cool whisper. Thierry started, then started again as he came unexpectedly out into the open, staring, craning his head back and back.

That? Dear saints, was that huge pillar soaring up into the sky really a tree? It was undeniably one of the most beautiful oaks he'd ever seen, tall and straight, those branches so far over his head, amazingly symmetrical, but the scale was just too overpoweringly huge for anything like mere human enjoyment. Thierry let out a long, wondering sigh. No oak—no tree of any sort—ever grew so mighty in his world!

Eh, wait. That first voice had probably belonged to a *lutin*, but the second certainly hadn't. "Forest Heart?" Thierry asked uneasily.

No answer. But amid the shadowy underbrush was one deeper shadow, and the faintest hint of glowing eyes. Their steady gaze sent a shiver through him, and Thierry heard himself chatter on. "It *is* you, isn't it? Of course, this is still forest, no matter how enchanted, so you'd still be a part of it, or it would be a part of you. Ah. I d-don't quite know what I'm saying. My—uh—my lord, do you know why I'm here?"

"Of course," whispered the inhuman voice. "What you seek is up there, up amid the highest branches."

"I . . . don't suppose you could . . ."

"No. That misenchanted, too-tall, ugly thing is none of mine. Magic spawned it, magic feeds it. It is a wrongness."

There wasn't the slightest rustle of leaves, and yet Thierry suddenly sensed the being was gone. He sighed, staring helplessly up the incredible height of the Oak to that distant, perfect crown of branches. A wrongness, indeed. No human could possibly climb that sleek trunk without spikes and a rope. Neither of which he had.

"Poor man, helpless man," mocked a shrill voice. "Can't even climb a tree."

Thierry was in no mood for teasing. "Neither could you," he snapped.

"Could! Could!"

Thierry tensed, suddenly inspired. "Oh, I don't believe you," he said, forcing lightness into his voice. "Everyone knows *lutins* never tell the truth."

"Do! We do!"

"Oh? I doubt that. Saying you could climb that tree . . ." Thierry folded his arms and turned away. "No. I don't believe you."

"Can too! Can too!"

"Prove it." Gambling that a magical being would be drawn to a magical object, Thierry added as casually as he could,

"Bring me . . . hmmm . . . bring me an acorn from the topmost branches."

There was the rustle of leaves, the scrape of claws. Thierry glanced subtly out of the corner of an eye to see a chestnut red squirrel—the *lutin*, surely—scrabbling up the Oak. He watched it climb up, up, till at last it was out of sight. Far overhead, leaves shook violently, then the squirrel came scampering down again, something clenched in its jaws. *The Acorn?* Thierry wondered nervously.

The *lutin* stopped just over his head, plainly at a loss as to what to do. It couldn't boast to the human while in squirrel form, certainly not with the Acorn clenched in its teeth. But it couldn't cling to the tree trunk in clawless *lutin* form, either!

Thierry didn't wait for it to unravel its confusion. "I don't believe that's really from this tree," he scoffed. "Looks like just any old nut to me!"

Insulted, the *lutin* started to chatter at him—only to have the Acorn pop free. Thierry snatched it up.

And in the next instant, he almost lost it again as a chaotic rush of sound, shape, wisdom poured into his brain. Hands shaking, Thierry fumbled with his belt pouch till he'd gotten it open, then hastily dropped the Acorn into it. Ah, saints, what a relief! The savage flood of knowledge was instantly cut off, leaving him with nothing worse than a pounding head.

But before Thierry could catch his breath, a great rush of wind hurled him off his feet. He twisted about just in time to see the Oak of Gwailahier snap out of reality.

Only the Acorn was holding it here! It took a moment for the spell to dissolve and—oh.

For the barest instant he glimpsed a strange, beautiful, terrifying land beyond the Oak, a land of clear, bright, sunless air and color just too clean and sharp to be Earthly, and knew from every tale he'd ever heard that he must be looking into true Faerie.

Then air rushed in with a roar to fill the space the tree had occupied, and Thierry flattened himself against the ground lest he be dragged after the tree, clinging frantically to roots till the sudden fierce wind was gone. Warily he got to his feet, brushing off twigs and earth.

"Well done."

"Forest Heart?"

"Well done," the soft voice repeated.

"Uh . . . thank you. But would you know where I—Forest Heart?"

He couldn't actually see any difference in the shadows, but somehow Thierry knew he was alone once more.

"Wonderful. *Now* where do I go?"

After the Jewel of Thought, of course, and the *guibre*. Whoever, whatever a *guibre* might be.

"Wonderful," Thierry repeated dourly.

All at once he flinched. The Acorn had suddenly given a sharp pulse, there in his belt pouch, almost as though reminding him of its presence. It wasn't a real acorn, of that there could be no doubt: a magical artifact of some sort, hidden for whatever devious Faerie reason amid the branches of an equally magical oak. But whatever it was, who or whatever had created it, surely something named the Acorn of Knowledge could tell him where to find the Jewel of Thought.

If he dared to use it. Hesitantly, the young man let his hand drop to the belt pouch. . . .

No! He couldn't face that flood of knowledge again! Thierry looked about in panic, hunting for Forest Heart, for a *lutin*, for anyone who might help him. But even the *lutin* seemed to have fled. Without a guide, he might wander these woods forever, and never find the Jewel, and never free Glinfinial.

"Oh, *damn!* Glinfinial, for you!"

Trying to think of the Jewel of Thought and only of the Jewel even though he hadn't the vaguest idea of what it looked like, Thierry closed his hand about the Acorn.

➢

Far from that place, looking into his magic mirror, Tiernathal let out his breath in a sharp hiss. The human had won the Acorn skillfully enough, but if he died now beneath the force of its Power. the thing would be as useless to anyone of Faerie as though it still hid amid the branches of the Oak. Yes, this forest was under Tiernathal's spells, but it was still rooted in the mortal world. Only if the Acorn was actually in Tiernathal's mansion, safely separated from any hint of alien-to-Faerie life, would the Faerie Lord have a chance of studying it in safety.

As a human could not.

"Curse you," Tiernathal whispered to Thierry, "curse you, *live!*"

Thierry heard himself cry out in anguish. Once again, he was overwhelmed by the wild rush of sight and sound and knowledge, more than any one merely human brain could hold—but this time, amid the chaos, he saw, he knew, the Jewel of Thought, and knew the perilous being that held it.

All at once it was beyond human endurance. Sobbing for breath, Thierry let the Acorn fall back into his belt pouch, then collapsed to his knees, hands to aching head.

Gradually the pain faded . . . faded. . . . It was gone. Thierry slowly surfaced back to sanity, realizing with a great surge of relief that he was himself once more, alone in his mind. After a moment, he struggled back to his feet.

And then, because there really was nothing else to be done, Thierry started forward once more.

He never heard Tiernathal's far-distant sigh of relief.

TWELVE

Guibre

"My lord."

Never taking his eyes from the magic mirror, Tiernathal waved a dismissive hand at the intruder. But rather than leaving, that intruder insisted in a tone sharp with anger, "My lord husband!"

He turned coolly, face schooled to show none of the impatience he felt. Nailaia and he had never been close, even from the early days of their marriage, and had been living apart ever since . . . Adele. Indeed, there were days Tiernathal could almost forget he *had* a wife! He certainly couldn't remember the last time she had actively sought him out.

"My lady wife," he said formally. "Nailaia. You will pardon me; I am occupied just now."

"Occupied!" One slender hand stabbed at the image in the mirror. "Occupied with yet another human!"

Tiernathal studied her, rather surprised at the small twinge of regret he felt at the sight. What a pity he didn't love her! Nailaia was an exquisite creature, her tall, slender figure hardly that of a woman who'd borne two children, the midnight blue of her gown a perfect foil for her pale, flawless skin. Her eyes were the careless color of the sky in spring, and coils of silvery blond hair crowned her head. If she had a flaw, the Faerie Lord mused, it was that she was so much younger than he, barely able to recall their native land, and still prone to outbursts of emotion.

Of jealousy?

"The human," Tiernathal said belatedly, "is my concern, not yours."

"Indeed? As that . . . half-blood child of yours is not my concern?"

Ah, that again! Jealousy indeed. Tiernathal frowned in warning. "Glinfinial is my daughter. You will accord her the courtesy you'd grant to your own children."

"Ae, husband, why must you be so *blind?* The girl is more human than Faerie, she always has been. She doesn't belong here, she can't belong here, and as long as she remains, she continues to be a source of turmoil."

"What nonsense."

"Haven't you *eyes,* husband? The girl rouses the worst, the most petty, behavior in our daughters! I've spoken to them about it, but until the cause is removed—Tiernathal, blood calls to blood. Let her go with her human boy and be happy."

"And be out of your reach, you mean!" The Faerie Lord hastily turned his attention back to the mirror, catching and sharpening the image just as it was about to fade. Staring at that image, he continued coldly, "She is, as you never fail to remind me, *my* daughter, mine alone. Her future lies in *my* hands, not yours. Leave me, Nailaia."

"Husband, please—"

"Leave me!"

"Tiernathal, look at me!"

As he turned back to her, stifling an impatient reply, Nailaia added softly, "I don't expect you to love me. You never have; we both know our marriage was for reasons of politics, back in—back in our own land, when such things had a meaning."

"Nailaia . . ." Tiernathal hesitated, not sure of what to say. "I'm sorry. You should never have agreed to wed me."

She spread her hands in a helpless gesture. "What choice had I? I was little more than a child. My lord, I'm not accusing you. You have never been anything but kind to me; I expected no more. Particularly once we came here, once I knew you'd given your heart elsewhere, to that . . . to the human woman."

Tiernathal fought to keep his voice even. "Nonsense. Wife, you're disturbing my magics. If you have nothing useful to say—"

"You *did* love her! As I . . . had come to love you . . ."

"Nailaia," the Faerie Lord repeated helplessly. "Don't . . ."

"Don't fear, my lord. I won't embarrass you with unseemly emotion. I only wish to add that I don't think you love anyone any longer, my lord. I don't think you can. Good day, my lord husband."

She swept from the room, but not before Tiernathal caught a suspicious trace of wetness on her cheeks. Stunned, he almost left the mirror to go after her.

And let the human escape him? And lose Glinfinial? Nailaia would soon be over this foolishness.

Schooling himself sternly to calmness, the Faerie Lord turned back to his mirror and his watching.

Crouching in underbrush, hardly daring to breathe, Thierry stared in wonder. The *guibre* was like nothing he had ever seen, beautiful and terrible in one, long and sleek as a serpent grown monstrously large as it drank from a forest pool, its scales softly glowing in the twilight like so many sheets of mother-of-pearl shrouded in mist. Twin horns framed its narrow, elegant head, curving up on either side of a crest that looked for all the world like a glistening silver crown. The *guibre*'s eyes were cold, clear silver: predatory eyes. Surely the safest thing to do would be simply to steal away before it caught sight of him and hope that, like Earthly snakes, it had no sense of hearing.

But of course, he couldn't do anything so sensible. There on the forehead of the *guibre*, set between the twin horns, glinted something that could only be the Jewel of Thought.

Of course. We can't have things too simple, now, can we?

As though it had heard his thoughts, the *guibre* raised its head to glance restlessly about, water dripping from its narrow muzzle. Thierry almost groaned aloud as he saw that what he had mistaken for mist were pale green wings.

A horned, winged predator. Thank you, Tiernathal, thank you very much!

But sarcasm wasn't going to get him anywhere. Warily, Thierry moved forward, a hunter stalking a hunter. If he could only climb one of those trees overhanging the pool, he just might be able to edge out along a branch and get close enough to snatch the Jewel of Thought—which did look rather loosely set in the creature's head—then, the good Lord willing, wriggle his way into underbrush too dense for the *guibre* to follow.

Assuming, of course, that the *guibre*, on top of everything else, didn't breathe fire. No. Any creature armed with sword-sharp horns like that didn't need flame as well.

Carefully, now, carefully . . .

He made it all the way up into a tree without the slightest cracking of a twig, edged his way out onto a branch . . . a little farther . . . only a little farther. . . . He could smell the *guibre* now, a dry, dusty smell mixed with a hint of spice. . . . A little farther . . .

Just as he reached out to snatch the Jewel, the *guibre* sneezed, for all the world like any other animal, jerking its head down. Thierry missed completely and crashed down into the pool with a yelp and a mighty splash. The *guibre* flinched away, then lunged. Thierry frantically floundered out, those deadly horns cutting the water like two scythes, barely missing him. He dove into the underbrush, the creature right behind him—and suddenly found himself out in the open, on the edge of a rocky grove. Heart racing, he glanced about for cover, but unless he could make it across the grove and into the stand of trees on the other side—

Inspiration struck. Thierry raced forward, hoping he wasn't going to trip over the broken ground, then whirled to yell, "Come on, you ugly thing! Couldn't catch a rabbit, you stupid excuse for a predator!"

The words, of course, meant nothing. But at the sight of its prey jumping up and down in defiance, the *guibre* screamed high and shrill as a storm wind and surged forward, wings spreading as it lunged. Thierry waited till the last possible moment, his heart pounding as though it were trying to leave his chest, then threw himself to one side. The *guibre* crashed into the trees.

And, as Thierry had prayed, those long, knife-sharp horns imbedded themselves in a tree trunk! The *guibre* shrilled its rage, twisting and squirming, wings beating in fury. The tree wasn't going to hold it trapped for long, so Thierry hurried forward, washed in the creature's hot breath, its fangs clashing so close to his face that his heart nearly stopped. Holding his own breath, he snatched the Jewel of Thought from its socket in the bony forehead—and he'd been right, it was only loosely embedded—dropped it into his belt pouch before it had a chance to do whatever it did, and scrambled off into the underbrush as fast as he could go.

At last, breathless and scratched, sure he'd fought and scrabbled his way across an entire forest, Thierry let himself sag to the ground, listening. . . .

Nothing. Or rather, nothing but the normal little forest sounds. Either the *guibre* was resting from its struggles, or it had decided to go after less unpleasant prey.

Thierry sat up, feeling his breath and heartbeat gradually slowing to normal. Hot, thirsty, and tired, he thought longingly of the *guibre*'s pool, which, for the few seconds he'd been in it, had felt wonderfully cool.

Might as well dream of walking on the moon!

Eh, well, he might as well see what he'd risked his life to grab. Thierry warily worked the Jewel of Thought out of his pouch into a fold of his sleeve so he could study his prize safely.

It didn't really look like a jewel at all now that he could see it up close, more like some clear, natural secretion that almost looked like the amber from far-off lands he'd seen at the Paris court.

If this is Tiernathal's idea of a jest . . .

No. He doubted that dour Faerie Lord had much of a sense of humor. Besides, whatever this Jewel might be, it must certainly hold magic within it, or there wouldn't have been that hint of eagerness in Tiernathal's voice.

Thierry touched the cautious tip of one finger to the Jewel, then drew it back with a gasp. Magic, all right, even if it hadn't flooded him with information like the Acorn of Knowledge. For the barest instant that he'd touched the Jewel, the whole world had seemed to reorder itself into a clear, perfectly rational arrangement of plant and mineral and flesh-and-blood, of thoughts far too rational for the human mind.

The young man hastily tipped the Jewel back into the belt pouch, hoping its magic wouldn't fight with that of the Acorn. If Tiernathal wanted the thing, he was welcome to it!

So now, two-thirds of this strange, strange quest done. Now he need only find the Pearl of Farsight.

"Only," Thierry said, and gave a weary laugh.

THIRTEEN

The Lady of the Moor

Thunderstruck, Tareniel and Serenial watched their mother rushing from their father's chambers.

"Why, she was weeping!" Tareniel exclaimed after a moment.

Serenial shivered. "And did you *feel* her aura? All sorrowing and furious and—and I don't know what else."

"You . . . don't suppose it was something we did, do you?"

"Something *she* did, more likely!" Serenial's toss of her head was in the direction of Glinfinial's bedchamber.

"But she's asleep!"

"Oh, she may be sleeping away like some little human ninny *now*—but who knows what she was up to before Father bespelled her!"

But for once they didn't enjoy slandering their half sister. "Why was Mother there?" Tareniel worried. "What could Father have said to her?"

"It must have been something dreadful."

"But why? What could Mother have done?"

"Worse, worse, what could he have done to Mother?" Serenial's voice quivered. "Wh-what if she's fallen out of his favor?"

Tareniel sniffed at her sister's formal wording. "She never was *in* his favor!"

"True, b-but we never saw her cry before, never! Something truly terrible must have happened between them!"

The sisters stared at each other in dawning panic. "If something's gone wrong between them," Serenial continued in a very little voice, "what happens to *us?*"

They fell silent, all at once too frightened to speak.

Never taking his eyes from the image in his magic mirror, Tiernathal carefully stretched stiff muscles in turn: neck, back, arms, and legs. Ahh, his eyes ached, too, his very *mind* ached from this constant watching! Once upon a time he could have banished fatigue with a Word. Now, with usable Power so faint in this accursed Realm, and growing ever fainter as far as his kind were concerned, it would take him more energy than it was worth to work even the slightest restorative spell.

Or to banish memory. His mind, stuck in its weary channel, insisted on repeating the sight of Nailaia storming into his chambers like some accusing spirit. Powers, who would ever have suspected that remote, formal young woman felt so strongly about him? Berating him on the subject of love, claiming he'd forgotten what it meant—what nonsense.

Too much idleness, that's what it must be. He must find her something productive to do, something to occupy her time and keep her from bursting in on him again with such a ridiculous attack.

But the pain in her eyes, the tears on her cheeks, had been so very real. . . . Tiernathal stirred uneasily. She was his wife, after all, the mother of two of his children. Why hadn't he tried to comfort her? Why couldn't he feel more than this vague regret?

Ah, nonsense indeed. If he'd abandoned the mirror, he would have lost the image he'd gone to such trouble to catch. Besides, love was for foolish youngsters, and he was far from being either. Nailaia must learn to accept that fact without any pampering from him!

Grimly, Tiernathal continued to stare into the mirror.

➢

Thierry awoke with a groan, slowly uncurling from his soggy bed of branches. Head in hands, he sat trying to get his brain to work.

Foolish me! I never realized there could be worse than mere twilight gloom.

For two days now this Faerie Realm had shown him its nastier side: For two days it had rained. And it hadn't been an honest, heavy drenching, here and gone again, the type of rain from which someone could take shelter, but a chill, steady mist that gave him no chance to really get dry, and left him shivering even when he managed to get a fire going.

Thierry got to his feet, stretching and twisting till he had thawed himself back to life. At least the rain did finally seem to be stopping.

Yes, of course. Give me just a tiny bit of hope. Just enough to drive me mad!

He could swear he had been trekking on and on and on for an infinity, his clothing growing increasingly disreputable, his beard now scraggly and annoyingly itchy. Yes, Thierry knew he still loved the forest, though that love was getting strained by dankness and wetness and that perpetual blue gloom. But oh, how he ached for home, his happy, living, *sunlit* home! Thierry shut his eyes, imagining a steaming hot bath, and himself soaking luxuriously in it. And afterward, sitting down to a dinner of warming, wonderful soup, yes, and a roast with the juices running out onto the platter. Dear God, he was sick of berries, of this quest, most of all of meekly having to do Tiernathal's bidding!

Then why do it?

Thierry stood as though turned to stone, stunned by his inner traitor self. But this endless questing, this cold and wet and gloom were surely more than a human should be expected to endure.

Why go on? Why not just give up?

"Glinfinial . . ."

But thoughts of love were so difficult to hold when he was

tired and cold and hopeless. If he surrendered here and now, he could go home, and be warm again, and dry, and fed.

And alone. Forever alone. As Glinfinial would be forever trapped.

"No . . ." Thierry groaned. "Ah, no . . ."

And what of Tiernathal? The count felt a hot little flame of anger stir within him at the thought. Ah, yes, Tiernathal! How the Faerie Lord would enjoy his surrender! Thierry could just picture him smiling at the sight of this lost, bedraggled human, saying scornfully, "*What else but surrender can you expect of such a weak little animal?*"

"This is all *your* doing, my lord," Thierry snarled at the distant Faerie Lord. "This quest, these perils—ha, for all I know, this rain is your creation, too!" For all he knew, Tiernathal couldn't hear a word he said, but it was wonderfully comforting to add a defiant, "Did you think you could shake my love for Glinfinial? You haven't. You won't. Curse you, you can't!"

Shouting was a mistake. His head still ached dully from the night before. Bah, of course it still hurt! He had once again been forced to turn to the Acorn of Knowledge or he'd never have learned where to find the moor the Lady of the Moor inhabited!

"You're welcome to the Acorn, the Jewel, and any other magical bit I might pick up along the way," Thierry told Tiernathal, whether or not the Faerie Lord could hear him. "And I hope the lot of them give you as much joy as they've given me!"

He kicked at a cluster of fallen leaves, and stifled a curse as his toe connected with a hidden rock instead. Limping a bit, Thierry trudged on.

As he traveled, Thierry saw that the flat, thickly forested land was beginning to change, sloping gently, then not so gently, upward. At last the young man had to scrabble his way up over roots and rocks, the forest thinning about him as he climbed. Trees gradually were replaced by shrub, shrubs by scraggly bushes.

I haven't climbed all that high, an abstracted corner of Thierry's mind noted. *The soil here must be too poor to support true forest. Like my birch-crowned hill.*

He let out a long, weary sigh. Lord, how he missed that hill! And the manor. And Gerard—what he'd give to hear one of the steward's lectures on propriety right now!—and old Simon and all the rest. No. He wasn't going to give in to homesickness again.

Finally Thierry staggered up onto the crest. He stood panting, catching his breath and glancing warily about, finding himself facing a panorama of rolling hills, desolate beneath the sunless twilight sky, their smoothness broken only by the occasional gnarly tree and carpeted by grass turned a sickly, unnaturally bright green by the weird light. A moor, all right, windswept and lonely.

Now all he had to do, Thierry thought with wan humor, was find the Lady who made this desolation her home. Easy. There could only be acres of empty land out there!

And yet . . . odd, how sure he felt that the right direction was this way. Thierry shrugged and boldly stepped out, striding along down the carpet of thick grass. Glancing down, he saw that the blades were long and broad, not quite like the grass of his world; with every step he took, they seemed to wrap softly about his ankles in a silky caress that sent an uneasy little prickle up his spine.

It's almost as though the grass wants *me to go this way!*

But that was impossible, wasn't it? A memory was teasing his mind, a memory of a story someone had once told him . . . Simon, probably . . . but he couldn't really remember it. . . . Without alarm, Thierry realized he couldn't really remember much of anything. It was much more comfortable not to think, just to stride along, the grass cushioning his feet, caressing his ankles . . . just to keep going toward the dip in the land that held enough water to qualify as a pool. Barren thing, that pool, clear gray-blue water beneath the gray-blue sky . . . The grass seemed to be leading him right toward the water and the one thin birch growing at its verge . . . right toward the water. . . .

Far from there, Tiernathal straightened, staring fiercely into the mirror. Ha! The young man had been snared at last! Now he'd meet his doom, and—

And the Acorn and Jewel would be lost with him. The Faerie Lord spat out a very unregal oath, calm shattered. How could he have been so foolish? How could he ever have let his insulted dignity get in the way of logic?

"Live, curse you!" he shouted at Thierry's image. "Wake up, you young human idiot, and *live!*"

"*Live!*"

It was the merest tickle in his mind, but it was just enough, like the touch of a spider strand against his face, to make Thierry start. His hand dropped against his belt pouch, loosening the cord, his fingers slipped inside, brushing the Jewel of Thought—and suddenly clear sense and memory shot back into his head.

God! This wasn't innocent, insensate grass! This was all one great organism, the predatory thing known in the old tales as *la mal herbe,* the Evil Herb. But while it had just enough conscious will to control and presumably lull into fatal collapse whatever prey was foolish enough to be snared by it, it didn't have enough strength to bring down anything as large as a human. It also didn't have much in the way of true intelligence, which meant that since he was being drawn in this one direction, the Evil Herb must surely be the tool of something else—

Some*one* else. As Thierry stared, she stepped soundlessly out from behind the birch tree. Like the tree, she was tall and gaunt, but there was a certain alien elegance to the inhumanly thin face with its high cheekbones and huge, staring eyes, a certain chill, terrible, primal beauty. There was no color to her at all: Her skin and wispy gown were white as the birch's bark, her long, loose hair whipped about her like black shreds of night. Her eyes . . . Thierry stared into their cold depths for a second, then, gasping with the effort, managed to tear his gaze away, uncertain of their hue—or even if they'd had a hue. Saints, saints, this was a being out of the same nightmare tale as the Evil Herb, this Lady of the Moor who meant to drain the life-force from him and toss what was left to the grass to devour, and he hadn't the vaguest idea how to stop her.

Because he didn't know what else to do, Thierry grabbed desperately at courtesy, bowing his most gracious bow.

"My lady, how honored I am to meet you!" To his relief, his voice quivered not at all. "I've heard tales of your beauty, but they all lied."

Thierry had a moment to wonder nervously if she understood the human language—or indeed, any language at all. But then:

"Lied?" Was there just the hint of surprise or annoyance in the chill, soft voice?

"Oh, yes, they all said you were beautiful but *only* beautiful, as though you were merely some empty-brained little maid. They didn't tell what a breathless wonder you are."

Which, he thought wryly, was true enough. A wonder she was, surely, and if she had her way, he'd be breathless!

"Indeed." The faintest trace of a smile touched the thin, pale lips. "You speak smoothly, human. You *are* human . . . yes. You fairly reek of mortality."

He didn't like the chill hunger glinting in those colorless eyes. "Uh . . . yes. I . . . uh . . . am human." *Stop blathering!* The longer he kept her talking, the less likely she was to kill him—he hoped—but Thierry couldn't find a thing more to say except . . . except, "But you're not going to kill me."

"Oh?" It was a coldly amused whisper. "Am I not? Why not, my brave human whom I could slay with a touch?"

She probably could do exactly that, Thierry thought, eyeing those white, long-fingered hands; her inhuman touch would probably freeze the blood in his veins.

"B-because . . ." he stammered. "Because I didn't come stumbling here like some mindless prey. Lady, you didn't need your Evil Herb to snare me."

"No? Are you going to say my 'breathless wonder' drew you?"

By God, she had a sense of humor! Even if no trace of it was warming those chill eyes.

"I wouldn't insult you with such easy words, lady," Thierry continued as confidently as he could. "But, truly, I *was* seeking you out. My story is an odd one. If I may continue? . . ."

To his relief, she waved a regal hand in consent. *Of course,* the young man realized, *living up here all alone with only the chance deer or whatever coming her way, she must be starved for conversation!*

All right. He'd tell her the whole story, the true story, and see what happened. . . .

". . . and so I had no choice," Thierry finished. "Right now, Glinfinial is the prisoner of—of her father." He was wary about actually naming Tiernathal, not sure whether or not this supernatural creature was the Faerie Lord's ally. "And the only way I can free her is to do her father's bidding."

" 'Her father,' " the Lady of the Moor echoed with a touch of impatience. "Who?"

The last thing he could afford was for her to become bored. Thierry admitted reluctantly, "The Faerie Lord Tiernathal."

"That one!" To Thierry's amazement, it was a cry of sheer cold rage. The Lady of the Moor's colorless eyes blazed and glittered like winter ice, her black hair snapped as though filled with its own life. "He dares meddle yet again!"

"Uh . . . lady?"

"What do you think I am doing here, in this eternal gloom? This is *my* tree, *my* pool, yet he has so enshrouded the land with his cursed Faerie spells that I am cut off from the rest of the world!"

"I—I see. I didn't realize—" Thierry began in wary sympathy, but she continued, raging in her cold fury.

"What am I to do here, what? No human comes this way, not shepherd, not lost traveler—there *are* no humans in this place, and so I must survive like a common predator! I, the Lady of the Moor, whom human folk once feared and revered, am forced to live on *vermin*, on what little animal lives *la mal herbe* can bring my way!"

"Oh," Thierry said feebly, thinking, so much for sympathy! "Ah. Well."

"So he wishes the Pearl of Farsight, does he?" All at once, the Lady of the Moor smiled without humor, her eyes so terrible that Thierry didn't dare meet their glare. "So be it! Take the Pearl, human. Do his bidding. Come, come, take it!"

For one heart-stopping moment, he thought she meant to touch him, and with that touch, kill him. But there wasn't anything else he could do, so Thierry held out his hand in desperate courage, heart pounding. To his relief, she merely dropped the Pearl into it.

Relief instantly turned to horror and Thierry gasped in involuntary pain. The Pearl, large, perfectly round, gleaming with its own light, was almost as bitterly cold as the lady's touch must be. Frantically Thierry fumbled with the belt pouch with his free hand, sure the Pearl was going to bite its icy way through his palm, sure he was never going to get the pouch open, sure he was about to lose his whole hand—

Ah, there, at last! With a shiver of relief, he dropped the Pearl into the pouch. Trying not to rub his red and aching fingers, hoping they weren't permanently frostbitten, he bowed again, shaking with cold.

"Th-thank you, lady."

She continued to smile her chill, angry smile. "You may thank me. He, the fool who imposes his will over others, he may not. Take the Pearl to the Faerie Lord Tiernathal, human. Let him see the truth-that-was and the truth-to-come and despair."

With a swirling of her white gown, she was gone, whether into the tree or the pool or thin air, Thierry couldn't say. He didn't wait to find out. Hastily, he turned and left, and this time the grass that slipped against his ankles made no attempt to stop him.

FOURTEEN

Confrontations

A gasp of sheer astonishment escaped Tiernathal's lips as he stared at the mirror.

The human had done it. He had actually won the Acorn, Jewel, and Pearl. He had survived even the Lady of the Moor—that chill, predatory creature—and now, by the terms of their pact, Tiernathal must release Glinfinial. Release her, and lose her to squalid humanity.

"No," the Faerie Lord whispered. "No. Curse him, he shall not have her. She shall not be so degraded."

Ah, but the Acorn, Jewel, and Pearl! Tiernathal shivered, knowing that for his people's sake he must have them, terrified that their Power, too, would fail him.

He must have them.

But if he accepted them, he lost Glinfinial.

Yet if he didn't lose Glinfinial, his people could never return to Faerie. They would continue to fade. If he didn't lose his daughter, it would be his people who were lost.

Tiernathal gave one sharp cry of despair. Instantly a hesitant servant, a delicate green-haired creature with wood-sprite blood clear in its ancestry, was at his shoulder, asking, "My lord?"

"Leave me," the Faerie Lord snapped.

"B-but, my lord, I heard—"

"Nothing!" Tiernathal sprang to his feet, realized even as

he did that he was taking out his frustration on an innocent servant. But as that servant cowered away, the Faerie Lord couldn't stop himself from shouting, "Get out of here, *now!*"

As the servant scurried away, Tiernathal sank back to his chair, staring blankly at the mirror.

What could he do to get out of this tangle? What could he possibly do?

As the servant scuttled down the mansion's hallways in a panic, a woman's voice called out, "Halt."

Ae, no! It whirled with a little squeak of dismay, shrinking back into a corner at the sight of the Faerie Lord's lady, eyes wide with fright.

"Oh, stop that," Nailaia said impatiently. "You know I'm not going to hurt you. What was happening in there?"

"I—I don't know, my lady."

"My husband cried out. *What happened?*"

The servant shrank back even farther. "I'm n-not sure."

"It had to do with the human, didn't it?"

"I—I think so. I think the human won. I think he found the three artifacts my lord charged him to find."

"Soo!" Nailaia breathed. She waved the servant away, hardly noticing how eagerly it scurried off. The human had won, had he?

That means my husband must honor his pledge. At last, oh, at last we shall be free of Glinfinial!

Ae-yi, ae-yi, first the Lord, then the Lady, and both of them fierce as wild things! The servant whimpered to itself, wanting nothing so much as to hide itself in the serenity of the mansion gardens. It had almost reached the first quiet greenness when a hand shot out and caught it by the shoulder. The servant turned, this time in weary resignation.

Of course. The way the day was going, who else would this be but the Lord and Lady's daughters?

"My ladies," it said quietly. "What would you?"

Tareniel released him. She exchanged a quick glance with her sister, then demanded, "What is Father doing?"

"No one will tell us *anything!*" Serenial added.

The servant quivered in renewed alarm. "If—if your lord father hasn't told you," it began carefully, "I d-don't know if I—"

"You will tell us," Tareniel purred. Her hand closed again on the thin shoulder. "Or we shall have you locked away in a little stone cell."

Locked amid dead stone? Locked away from greenery? "No, no!" the servant pleaded. "Not that, please!"

Head hanging, it told them of the Tests posed, the Tests achieved. As Tareniel and Serenial glanced at each other again, eyes wide with surprise, the servant took advantage of their confusion to scuttle away; diving into the security of a thick rosebush.

Surrounded by vegetable calm, the servant curled up into a comfortable ball. Gradually the rapid beating of its heart slowed to tranquility. The servant shook its head. Such a fuss over mere humans! Well, now, soon enough the full human and the half human would be gone, and maybe then there wouldn't be all these tensions and alarms. For what else could the Faerie Lord do, hate it though he might, but honor his Faerie oath?

Thierry looked about the forest in growing rage. He'd expected something to happen once he had the three magical items, something dramatic, something magical, but not even a leaf had stirred. What now? Was this whole thing nothing but some Faerie jest? Or was he supposed to find the Faerie Lord all by himself? His quest was done, but he hadn't the vaguest idea where to go now.

I am not *going to use the Acorn of Knowledge again! I've had enough headaches on Tiernathal's behalf.*

The Faerie Lord wanted these objects? Fine! Let him come and get them! Thierry told himself that, come what may, he was not going to do any more weary trudging!

"Tiernathal!" he bellowed. "Tiernathal! You're listening, aren't you?"

There was a brief rustling in the undergrowth, a stirring in the trees, then silence.

"Come on, Faerie Lord, I know you must be listening!"

He was beginning to feel very foolish, shouting like this into empty forest.

"Very well, hear me! I have the Acorn, the Jewel, and the Pearl—and if you want them, you can just come and get me!"

The echoes settled. Almost total silence fell over the forest once more, broken only by the whisper of a breeze through the treetops. Thierry had just about decided he'd wasted his breath—

—when he felt himself seized by what felt like a giant, invisible hand. He had just enough time to think, *Now, what?* and hope it wasn't Tiernathal's way of getting rid of him before—

—the world disappeared into a rainbow swirl of color. There was no *up* or *down*, no sound or sensation other than—

Thierry grunted with the sudden impact of *solid* beneath his feet. He was here. Wherever "here" was. As full weight returned to him, he staggered, blinking till the world came back into sharp focus.

Uh . . . well . . . I did see him whisk Glinfinial away; he must have just done the same thing to me. I . . . think I prefer plain old walking!

All around him were the walls of what could only be Tiernathal's estate: towering white things engraved with intricate traceries of gold. He stood within a small garden, each bush eerily identical to the next, the sweetness of roses in his nostrils.

A . . . being was facing him. Slight and not quite reaching to his shoulder, it could have been either a girl or a very young man, and its long, silky hair was quite definitely green.

"What—ah, who are you?" Thierry managed.

The being shook its head. "Human," it said.

"Uh, yes, I'm human. But who brought me here? It couldn't have been you, could it? Where is—"

"Human," it repeated, clearly uncomfortable with this unfamiliar language. "Come. Bathe."

"Wait. Where's Tiernathal? And Glinfinial! Where is she?"

The being only stared.

"Oh, come, you must understand something of what I'm saying!"

"Something."

"Oh, wonderful! Isn't there anyone in this place who speaks the—uh—the human language?" Thierry stopped short. Why should they? This was hardly a human place. He took a deep breath and said, very precisely, "Tiernathal. Take—me—to—Tiernathal."

That, the being seemed to have understood. But its contemptuous gaze said without words, Not as you are! Suddenly very much aware of his disreputable appearance, Thierry remembered the elegant Faerie Lord, not a fold of clothing out of place, and sighed again, this time in resignation.

"Bathe," he agreed wryly.

Tiernathal groaned, slowly dragging himself up from the floor. Ae, Powers, that had been an effort! Bad enough to hurl his daughter from *there* to *here*; she was, after all, linked to him by blood, making things easier. But there'd been no possible link with the human, and with the three magical artifacts fighting him . . . He shuddered, then winced, raising a hand to an aching head. Fortunate he'd sent someone to meet the man and delay him. No one, least of all a human, was going to see a Faerie Lord in such a sorry state. Faugh, and he stank of perspiration, too!

Nostrils flared in distaste, Tiernathal summoned a servant to bathe and dress him. As the being fussed over the folds of an elegant, midnight blue tunic and cloak, the Faerie Lord asked thoughtfully, "Is the human still engrossed in being cleaned? Yes? Then bring me the pouch you will find with his discarded clothing."

As the being hurried off, Tiernathal straightened regally, face composed. Not a human born could have read the anticipation, the near terror, behind that quiet mask.

Some time later, that mask was shattered. Alone in his workroom, the Acorn, Jewel, and Pearl before him, Tiernathal clenched his teeth and fought to keep from shrieking. Fool, oh fool! Why hadn't he realized what was going to happen? By not giving the human any manner of guide, he'd forced the man to rely on the Acorn. And by using it, he had, all unknowing, repatterned the thing with his own aura! Oh, the Acorn still held Knowledge—but Knowledge so overlaid with humanity that it was useless to anyone of Faerie!

And the Jewel—ah, the Jewel! It hadn't been as badly tainted, though the touch of humanity swirled all through it. But the clear Thought Tiernathal had been able to wrest from it was stupid, useless, telling him only that wisdom lay in sending Glinfinial away.

"No," he whispered fiercely. "That shall not be!"

There was still the last of the three, the Pearl of Farsight. Barely daring to hope, Tiernathal closed his hand on it, opening his mind to whatever it would show him. . . .

And what it showed him was the past, Adele, his lovely Adele . . . his Adele growing wan and weak . . . his Adele . . . dying . . . dying despite all his magic . . . dying. . . .

And what it showed him was the future, Glinfinial, his only tie with Adele . . . Glinfinial scorning him . . . deserting him . . . as Adele had deserted him . . . Adele . . .

Tiernathal surfaced, gasping as though he'd run a terrible race. He blindly hurled the Pearl from him, not caring what became of it. The Lady of the Moor had done this, tricked him, nearly trapped him, curse her, and there was no way back to Faerie, none!

Just at that moment, there was a wild commotion at the

door. It burst open, and in stormed the human, frantic guards trying to stop him, a crowd of curious courtiers in their wake. Thierry had been bathed and shaven; clad in proper Faerie tunic and cloak, he looked almost civilized. But there was nothing civilized about his raging aura, nor about the way he shouted out, "You thief! Couldn't you even wait for me to give them to you?"

Still stunned by shock and grief, Tiernathal could only counter with a lame, "They were not yours to keep."

"All right, then, forget that!" the human snapped. "I don't care what you do with the things! I passed your Tests, you can't deny it. Now free Glinfinial and let us go!"

. . . Glinfinial scorning him, deserting him . . . as Adele had deserted him . . . Adele dying . . . Glinfinial . . .

"No!" Tiernathal gasped, and then, more rationally, "Not just yet."

Thierry stiffened. "But you gave your word! You promised that Glinfinial and I would be free!"

"No, I—I never said that." Thinking frantically, remembering his exact words, the Faerie Lord added, "Not exactly. I only said that you and she would be safe. And safe, you both undeniably are."

"Why, you *liar!* You oath breaker!"

The Faerie folk gasped in horror, guards clamping down on Thierry's arms. Weapons flashed—

"Enough!" Tiernathal thundered. "The human knows no better. Release him."

"But my lord," argued one of the guards, "to accuse you of—of . . . untruth!"

He said the word with loathing, like the Faerie obscenity it was, but there was an uneasy glitter in his eyes, in the eyes of them all, that made Tiernathal wince. His own mind was echoing, *Liar. Oath breaker.* No, curse it, he *wasn't* a liar, none of it was a lie! And yet, and yet, if he didn't do something to stop this insanity now, the story was going to spread among all his people—

"I never promised to free you," he said to the human as

coolly as he could. "But I am familiar with your human concept of mercy. And so I will give you one last chance. You shall attempt to single out Glinfinial from among all the maidens. If you can do that one small task, then shall you both be free!"

Thierry eyed him dubiously, plainly suspecting a trick, and Tiernathal tensed. What if the human dared refuse him? What, then?

But at last the young man nodded. "So be it. A warning, though, my lord: no more games. A promise, as well: No matter how you hide my love, I shall find her. And I, my lord," he added dryly, "am no oath breaker."

Why, you arrogant little worm! For a long, tense moment, Tiernathal battled to keep himself from striking down the human where he stood. But that would only reinforce the rumor that he had broken his word, so the Faerie Lord contented himself with saying only: "Shall you?" *I'll see you dead first, you puny thing, you source of all my trouble.* "Shall you indeed?"

FIFTEEN

The Choosing

Glinfinial stirred groggily. Sleepy . . . she was so sleepy . . . but she'd already slept for . . . for . . . How long *had* she been asleep? It didn't really matter. . . . Nothing mattered. . . . It was so comfortable not to have to think or move or do anything but just drift back into the warm, heavy darkness. . . .

"Glinfinial!"

A voice was hissing in her ear, weaving its way into her dreams. She whimpered, trying to slip back into peace.

"Glinfinial, wake up!"

"Mmm . . ." It was too much of an effort to form words, but she must, because that voice was insisting.

"Wake up, girl!"

"No . . ." she managed. "Go 'way. . . ."

"Glinfinial! We don't have time for this—Glinfinial!"

A hand smacked against her cheek, once, a second time. It hurt! Angrily, Glinfinial forced open heavy eyelids to see:

"Nailaia! My lady Nailaia! What? . . ."

"Here, sit up. Gently, now!" Nailaia supported her with brusque efficiency until Glinfinial could manage for herself.

"How . . . how long was I asleep?"

Nailaia snorted. "Long enough, thanks to *him*."

Glinfinial warily tried swinging her legs over the edge of the bed, feeling the mists shrouding her mind slowly drifting away, bit by bit. "Him? You mean Father?"

"Of course your father! Don't you remember?" Nailaia stood, the very image of barely controlled nerves.

"He . . . bespelled me, didn't he? Yes! Now I remember! I tried to fight back, but he was just too strong."

"Hmph! Bespelled you, then was so proud of his handiwork he thought no one else could lift the spell, not even his wife! Come, get up. We have to get you out of here before your father finds out what happened."

"But Thierry—"

"Is here in the mansion. That's right, here."

"Then he—he completed that quest Father set him on, and we're free to leave!"

"Hardly. Oh, he completed the quest, all right. But your father isn't so ready to yield. He plans to set your young man some manner of ridiculous test he can't possibly win."

"But—but that's not right!" Glinfinial protested. "Didn't Father give his word to let us go? He would never have broken that—"

"Never mind, never mind." Nailaia wouldn't meet her gaze. "If we move quickly, we can have you two out and safely away."

She reached for Glinfinial's arm, but Glinfinial pulled away. "Why are you helping us? My lady, you and I have never exactly been friendly."

"We've never been enemies either. Look you, girl, I'm not some foolish human, to blame you for your father's straying. But you don't want to stay here, do you?"

"No, of course not."

"And I don't want you to stay here. So there we are. Now, hurry!"

"I think not," said a cold voice.

"Husband!" gasped Nailaia, and "Father!" exclaimed Glinfinial. He stood in the doorway like some figure of sorcerous menace, tall and fierce, his aura sharp with the Power of a spell just barely held in check.

"Leave us, wife. And you, daughter: I have need of you."

"Well, I have nothing to do with you! You broke your word!"

"Be still."

Fuming, Glinfinial tried to elude him, to fight back, but he had already completed the spell he'd been holding ready, and hurled it at her. She had time for one savage, "Oath breaker!"

And then magic enfolded her yet again.

How long she had been lost in an enchanted mist, Glinfinial had no way of knowing. But when her mind finally cleared, she was hard put not to scream in horror. She was trapped, totally trapped, in a close, close prison! Unable to move, barely able to breathe what air filtered in to her, at first the only thought penetrating her fright was that her father had buried her alive. No, no, he'd never do a thing like that!

Not exactly. At last Glinfinial realized what had happened: Tiernathal, as once before, had imprisoned his daughter in a tree.

While Tiernathal was out creating his new Test, Thierry thought, the human was being left to cool his heels. Or rather, he was being allowed to wander as he would, as though he were a child or some harmless pet, never quite coming face to face with any of the folk he knew were watching him.

What he saw struck him as being almost . . . sad. Thierry had imagined that a Faerie mansion would be a place of magical splendor, with glistening walls and soaring towers. There weren't any towers here, or anything of Otherworldly grace. Oh, the furnishings—the chairs and tables and tapestries—looked elegantly alien from afar, but seen up close, he realized they were so poorly made as to be almost shoddy.

Thierry shook his head. Whenever these folk had made the crossing from Faerie to here, they'd obviously neglected to include craftsmen. And with Tiernathal's prejudices against humankind, he certainly wouldn't have hired any mortal workers!

Sadder still, what bits of wonder he did find, like those beautifully inlaid walls, the golden pattern much more delicate and intricate than anything wrought by human hands, showed, on closer examination, sorry signs of tarnish and wear that surely didn't belong in the home of a magical people.

They're fading, he realized with a shock, *Tiernathal's folk and their magic are fading. Even if they still have enough strength to hold this Realm in twilight, it's just a matter of time before that spell breaks and it all ends for them.*

To his surprise, he found himself almost pitying the Faerie Lord. There was Tiernathal trying so fiercely to pretend all was well, holding so desperately to his prejudices and his pride: Surely he saw what was happening to his people, and must be anguished over his inability to stop it.

"Human." It was the servant who'd led him to the baths. "Come."

He followed the inhuman guide out beyond the mansion walls to where the Faerie Lord waited, cold face impassive, a whole horde of guards and courtiers and servants—all his people, come to watch this test of Faerie against human—gathered behind him, in a narrow meadow lined with young birch trees. Thierry shrugged mentally, decided on courtesy, and gave Tiernathal a low, sweeping bow.

"My lord."

He received the smallest nod of the head in return. "You are ready for your testing?"

"I'd better be, hadn't I?"

"Then—choose." The Faerie Lord's sweep of arm took in the entire row of birches.

"I . . . uh . . . beg your pardon?"

"One of those trees is not a tree. One of them is Glinfinial. Choose, human. Find my daughter."

"*What?* But—but only a magician could do that!"

Tiernathal raised one elegant eyebrow. "Do you surrender, then?" he purred.

"No, curse you, I don't!"

"Well?"

Ignoring the man as best he could, Thierry walked slowly down the row of trees, his spirits sinking ever lower as he examined them. Tiernathal really did mean to destroy him, because each birch was absolutely the same as the next, bark, branch, and leaf. There were too many in the row for him to risk simply picking one at random and hoping for the best. But what else could he do? Without magic, how could he possibly win?

"I won't give up," Thierry muttered. "Glinfinial, Windleaf, where *are* you?"

Dimly, Glinfinial was aware that someone was calling her name. Dimly, she sensed . . .

Thierry! My love, my love, I'm here!

If only she could scream that out! But not a sound could penetrate this close prison. Heart racing, Glinfinial could *feel* Thierry passing slowly back and forth before her, tormentingly close, and yet there wasn't anything she could do about it! She knew what her father must have done—how could she have forgotten that other imprisonment in that other birch tree?—she knew her prison was only one of a row of trees, almost certainly identical trees. Soon Thierry would have to choose, and choose at random. And if his pick was wrong, they were both lost.

Oh, Thierry, no, no!

She fought against her father's spell as fiercely as ever a wild thing battled the cage imprisoning it—and as uselessly. Exhausted, Glinfinial wished she had enough breath to weep, or scream out her rage.

Wait . . . What happens if I don't *fight the spell, not exactly? Yes . . . what if I simply . . . sidestep it?*

She couldn't escape on her own. That left only one possible thing for her to do. Glinfinial drew all her mental strength to her, gradually narrowing her thoughts to just this one thing, this one thing that must be done, focusing her will and hurling it forth to change, change. . . . Her heart was pounding painfully, her lungs were laboring in the not-quite-enough air, her head—Ae, her head! This wasn't going to work, it would never work, her brain was going to burst first!

No! She would *not* doubt. Doubt destroyed magic, and this was such a small magic: She could do this, she would!

And suddenly Glinfinial had it. Suddenly she felt the smallest bit of the outer reality . . . change.

Enough. I—I just can't do any more. Now it's up to Thierry and his woodcraft. Be wise, my love, for both our sakes, be wise!

Thierry walked up and down the row of trees again and yet again, studying each one with agonizing care. Surely there must be *some* difference, surely he'd sense his lady even as things were. But no matter how he looked, there simply wasn't any difference in any of them. Nor could he sense anything special about any of the trees.

There has to be something!

Clenching his fists, he started down the line once more. Somewhere off in the forest, a hint of darker shadow amid shadow told him that Forest Heart was watching him.

"Don't just look at me," Thierry said under his breath. "*Do* something." But he'd never yet seen the being leave the shadows, and apparently nothing was going to change that fact now. "So much for repayment of debts."

Although Tiernathal hadn't said a thing during all this time, Thierry knew it couldn't be much longer before even that Faerie being began to lose patience. He was very much aware of the Faerie Lord, there at the fringes of his vision, triumph glinting in the cold green eyes.

"Stare all you want," Thierry muttered. "You haven't got me, not yet."

Oh, right. Defiance was all well and good, but it was surely just a matter of time before—

Hey, wait! What was . . .

Thierry looked, and looked again, hardly daring to hope. And then he let out a great roar of laughter. If he hadn't been so familiar with the woodland, he might never have noticed, but there it was: All the birch trees *had* been absolutely the same—yet all at once this one was sporting one tiny *oak* leaf!

"Glinfinial!" he cried, and dimly felt her mind brush his own. "Yes, yes, *yes!*" He whirled to face Tiernathal, shouting, "Here she is, Faerie Lord! Here is my own dear lady!"

SIXTEEN

Debts Repaid

"Here she is, Faerie Lord! Here is my own dear lady!"

As Thierry's triumphant shout tore through the still air, the spell Tiernathal had laid upon his daughter shattered. The one false birch tree among the true fell apart into shards that just as swiftly faded into mist. Disheveled and laughing breathlessly, Glinfinial stumbled free. Thierry enfolded her in his arms, and they clung to each other, too breathless for speech, as though they would never again be parted.

"No-o-o!"

It was a shriek of raw fury from Tiernathal. Thierry and Glinfinial whirled in shock, still arm in arm, to be faced with the Faerie Lord, whose icy calm had at last splintered. Elegant face contorted by rage and pain, eyes blazing with green fire, Tiernathal shouted, "You have not won, human! You are the oath breaker, not me! Fool, dishonorable fool, you have cheated!"

"Why, I—I did nothing of the sort!" Thierry gasped out, too stunned by this sudden hysteria to do anything but clutch Glinfinial protectively to him. Flashes of all he'd undergone went through his mind: the Tarasque, the Lady of the Moor, all the weary, hopeless hours of wandering, and he almost burst into fury of his own. But that would be a perilous thing to do, so he managed to simply state, biting off each word savagely, "You told me to bring you the Acorn, the Jewel, and the Pearl, and so I did. You told me to pick my lady out of that row of trees, and so I did. There wasn't anything dishonorable about any of it!"

"And you're hardly the one to speak of cheating, Father!" Glinfinial added sharply, her own eyes ablaze. "You, who imprisoned your own child just because she happened to fall in love!" She glanced at Thierry. "But we're willing to forget, Thierry and I, and I to forgive. Just give us permission to leave."

"You *dare!*" Tiernathal's voice was thick with anger. "You defiant little wretch! No, you shall *not* have permission! You are my daughter, you are mine, and you shall learn to obey me!" His fiery gaze shot back to Thierry. "And you, you lying, dishonorable human fool, you have betrayed me—and I shall have your life!"

Sudden magic crackled in the air around him, sharp and deadly. But just as suddenly: "Oh, I think not," said a quiet voice, and everyone there started. A shadow darker than the shadows of the forest had somehow slid out from that forest and was moving silently from birch to birch.

Tiernathal was the first to recover. "Forest Heart!" he hissed. "Begone! This is none of your affair!"

"But it is," the being corrected coolly. "I care little for your kind, Faerie man—or, to be honest, for humankind, either. But this young man, human though he may be, has proven himself a forest-friend, a fire slayer. He has put me in his debt." The birches swayed slightly, their branches stirring though there was no wind as Forest Heart continued softly, with just the barest hint of menace. "Unlike you, Faerie man. I have grown weary and weary again at seeing your people use the forest's own sweet trees for their magics."

"I am not your subject!" Tiernathal snarled. "And I say the human shall die!"

"Indeed?" Forest Heart murmured, moving yet closer to where Thierry and Glinfinial stood. Thierry stared, but even now could make out no more detail than hint of claw, hint of feather. "Tell me this, young things," the being said. "Do you truly love each other?"

"Of course we do!" they answered, almost as one, and Thierry added, "Do you think I would have gone through all that stupid questing if I didn't?"

The soft rustling might have been a chuckle. "No. I doubt you would. But tell me this, young things: what if it came to the edge of death for you? Would you sacrifice yourselves, one for the other?"

Thierry and Glinfinial glanced at each other. "I would," Thierry said softly. "I'd rather live, if it's all the same to you, but yes, I would die for my lady if need be."

"And I," Glinfinial added firmly, "would glady give up life itself to know Thierry alive and happy."

"Oh, my dear," Thierry gasped, "how could I ever, ever be happy without you?"

"Or I without you?"

"You see?" Forest Heart said to Tiernathal, and behind the simple words blazed the elemental joy that was the forest's ever-new life.

As the young people embraced yet again, Tiernathal cried out once more, this time in pain, seeing with eye, *feeling* with mind, the love blazing up between them, all bright and brave and wonderful. It was too strong to endure, it was fire beyond bearing, burning at barriers, burning at memory, forcing him to see himself then, himself now, and realize:

Adele, oh, my dear Adele, I never hated what you were, never. I loved you! I loved you!

Ae, yes, he had loved her as fiercely as those two young things clinging desperately to each other. But she had died. Adele had betrayed him by dying. And he, the Faerie man knowing nothing of mortality, had been so terrified of his own reaction, of the unfamiliar pain of grief, that he'd mistaken it for weakness. He'd forced himself to be ashamed. He'd banished warmth and memory and . . . himself . . . behind a wall so thick that no pain could ever reach him.

Nailaia was right, Tiernathal realized, shaken, *I really had forgotten how to love. I had forgotten how to* live!

He glanced at his wife, who stood to one side, staring at the young couple with envy and anguish plain in her eyes. Tiernathal hesitantly called her name, and Nailaia turned to look at him, her aura aching with such pain and longing that he could only remember her words, "I had come to love you," and wonder, *Could it still be? Oh, maybe . . .*

Hardly daring to dare, Tiernathal held out a pleading hand to her. Nailaia wordlessly came into his arms, warm against his chest, and he—

—felt the last ice melt within him and he—

—could remember everything, *everything*, the knowledge he'd locked away with his refusal to mourn, the knowledge that told him—

"Yes, oh yes! How could I ever have forgotten?"

Tiernathal cast out a hand, laughing, calling.

And the Gate shimmered into being, as easily as a door swinging open, and Faerie lay beyond it.

"We can go home!" Tiernathal's voice rang with joy. "My people, my people, can you ever forgive me? Can you forgive me for the foolishness that held us here so long? At last we can go home!"

Thierry felt Glinfinial shudder in his arms. He looked up to see the Gate, and beyond it a hint of that most wonderful, most terrible land he had glimpsed when the Oak had been drawn through. Faerie, dear God, Faerie, and Tiernathal's folk were joyously slipping back into it, one by one. As he watched, Tareniel and Serenial passed through, glancing back at their sister with unreadable glances that just might have been pitying.

Pity? Oh, God, they expect her to come with them, to leave me and be truly of Faerie, and she . . .

But he couldn't bear to continue the thought, seeing the inhumanly bright light blazing in her eyes.

Now only the Faerie Lord and his Lady were left. Nailaia

touched her husband's arm in a gentle caress, then passed through the Gate with a wondering smile. But Tiernathal hesitated right on the verge of the Gate to turn back to Thierry and Glinfinial.

"I have wronged you both greatly. Will you forgive me?"

After a moment, Glinfinial nodded. What could Thierry do but agree? The Faerie Lord dipped his head to them in grave dignity. But strain was plain on the elegant face, and his voice quivered slightly when he added, "I cannot hold the Gate open much longer. Glinfinial, there can be no delay. You must decide this moment which Realm shall be yours."

Oh, God, thought Thierry again, *I'm going to lose her. After all this, I'm going to lose her.*

But Glinfinial shook her head. "I have already chosen," she said softly. "Live ever in joy, Father."

For one long moment, the Faerie Lord stared into his daughter's steady gaze. Then the faintest of smiles touched his lips. "Live ever in joy, Glinfinial," he murmured, and sprang through the Gate.

It closed behind him as smoothly as though it had never been. With its closing, the twilight spell dispelled as quickly as mist before the sun. As the land brightened into daylight about them, Glinfinial collapsed into Thierry's arms, clinging to him, burying her head against his chest, trembling so violently that surely only his grip was keeping her from falling. Feeling impossibly helpless, he couldn't think of anything to do but stroke her hair, murmuring broken phrases of comfort, enjoying the warm, soft feel of her but aching with sympathy. He could almost stand like this forever, his lady in his arms. . . .

But at last Glinfinial pulled away from him, eyes quite dry. "Well," she said noncommittally.

"Well," Thierry echoed, then added falteringly, "shall we . . . shall we go home?"

To his relief, she didn't even hesitate. "Oh, yes!"

But as they started forward, arms around each other,

Thierry couldn't stop tormenting himself. He'd taken her away from her family, her people—well, no, she'd *chosen* to leave them, there was that, but still . . . Would Glinfinial truly be happy now? Could she be? Wouldn't she miss the Realm of magic?

Almost as though she'd sensed his thoughts, Glinfinial gave a sudden chuckle. Surprised, Thierry glanced at her to see a hint of magic still flickering in his love's green eyes. Why, of course! Her people might be back in Faerie, but she still possessed her own powers.

"Look, love," she teased.

Glinfinial held out her hand to him. A bright green rose suddenly lay across her palm, so clear an illusion that dew drops glistened on its velvet petals, then, just as suddenly, vanished into air again. Glinfinial grinned at him, her eyes full of mischief. Thierry, heart wild with joy, grinned back.

Their life together certainly wasn't going to be dull!